THE PANDORA PARADOX

AN EROTIC MYSTERY NOVEL

Jane Grey

Battle Press
SATELLITE BEACH, FLORIDA

THE PANDORA PARADOX

Battle Press books may be ordered through booksellers or by contacting:

Battle Press
1-919-218-4039
steve@battlepress.media
www.battlepress.media

ISBN: 979-8-9905619-4-6 (softcover)
ISBN: 979-8-9905619-5-3 (eBook)
LCCN: 2024923042

First Edition.

Pan-do-ra   [pan'dora]

The first mortal woman. In one story she was created by Zeus and sent to earth with a box of evils in revenge for Prometheus' having brought the gift of fire back to the world. Pandora kept out all evils from the box to infect the earth; hope alone remained to assuage the lot of humans.

Par-a-dox   [pera'daxs]
Noun

1.   One (such as a person, situation, or action) having seemingly contradictory qualities or phases.

2.   A statement that is seemingly contradictory or opposed to common sense and yet is perhaps true (incongruous).

Merriam-Webster Dictionary
2020 Edition

Author's Note

When I was asked to write this story, I had serious misgivings. The mystery behind the plot certainly makes for an interesting story; one that most mystery/detective fans would find very appealing. At the same time, sexuality is an essential ingredient of the story.

Unfortunately, or fortunately - depending on one's viewpoint toward erotica - the narrative may prove offensive. This was my conundrum when considering whether or not I would write the story. I determined at the outset, there was no good way to tell this story without explicit description of the numerous sexual situations essential to the plot. Thus, for me, as an author, it became all or nothing. Obviously, I have chosen the former.

At its heart this is a quest, impossible that it may be, to explore the limits of sexual desire and the benefits and/or *consequences* of uninhibited sexual behavior. An experimental aphrodisiac dubbed *Pandora* is the catalyst that sets in motion the events depicted in the novel. With one obvious exception, the characters of the story are all (like the rest of us) a blend of good and bad. On which side of the equation, they eventually land…well, that's up to the reader to decide.

The person who created this story wanted it told from a feminine point of view. I've done my best to accomplish that mandate. Before concluding, I would like to acknowledge the person that created this unique story. I am honored for being tasked with putting pen to paper, ultimately bringing this novel to fruition.

Jane Grey

Primary Characters

Reference List

Brick Winstone	Chief of R&D for Delta Pharma. Created aphrodisiac drug *Pandora*
Benedict Winstone	New Hampshire Senator; Brick's father
Judith Winstone	Brick's mother; struggling to improve inadequate love life
Molly Skye	Research Assistant; First test subject for *Pandora* drug trial
Ted Dixon	Brick's best friend; Molly Skye's fiancée
Dana Bryce	Brick's Secretary; member of Molly's Clique
Sue Alverez	Controls drug inventory: member of Molly's Clique
Allison McKenna	Delta Pharma Chief Accountant; member of Molly's Clique
Matthew McNeil	CEO of Delta Pharma; Good friend of Senator Winstone
Endora McNeil	Matthew's wife; Good friend of Judith Winstone
Sean Wilder	Chief Investigator, D.A. Office; Robyn Wilder's husband
Robyn Wilder	Private Investigator; Sean Wilder's wife

Kris Wood	Psychiatrist; Best friend of Robyn/Sean Wilder; lives with Tom Clipper
Tom Clipper	E.R. Physician; Best friend of Robyn/Sean; lives with Kris Wood.
Jean LeFleur	Carpenter; shady past; befriended by Sadie Adams
Sadie Adams	Independent middle-aged prostitute; befriends Jean LeFleur
Richard Daughtery	Manchester Police Chief; Friend of Senator Winstone, Matthew McNeil
David Wozniak	Hillsboro D.A.; Boss/Friend of Sean; Friend of Chief, Senator
LeBron Smith	Manchester Police Chief Detective; good friend of Sean Wilder
Robert Landry	Senator Winstone's Press Secretary; Judith Winstone's lover
Patricia O'Brien	Murdered prostitute; Sadie Adams had tried to help with her addiction
George Tylor	Senator Winstone's Chief of Staff; Bandy Tylor's father.
Bandy Tylor	George's daughter. Youngest to be exploited by Brick

Chapter One

Matthew McNeil set the packet of five pills down on his desk, then leaned back in his chair. Bringing his hands together to form a steeple, he looked up, fixing his gaze on one Brick Winstone, the new boy-wonder of Delta Pharma, Ltd.

"So, Brick, tell me again what this hormonal modifier is going to do for Delta Pharma."

Brick Winstone is the son of long-time New Hampshire Senator Benedict Winstone. He is very bright - a member of Mensa - and has degrees in both law and pharmaceuticals. To his father's chagrin, he developed a reputation as a ne'er-do-well playboy; constantly having run-ins with law enforcement, necessitating his father's frequent interventions to stay out of the headlines.

Unfortunately for Brick, he wasn't particularly attractive to women, at least the pretty ones, the *only* ones he liked. Fortunately for Brick - as a Winstone he had lots of money and spent it freely on wooing the pretty ones. But Brick had a quirk. Sexual satisfaction for him was largely dependent on his perception of how much his partner *really* desired him. He could spot a fake orgasm a mile away. His quirk turned out to be the catalyst for his developing this newest aphrodisiac.

"Once we've verified its effectiveness, the company will make millions in profit," promised Winstone.

"Ah, but there's the rub," replied McNeil, beginning to fidget with the packet, "It's going to take months, if not years, in clinical studies before we can market it. You know the company's financial situation - we need lots of capitol - NOW."

"I have a solution," said Winstone. "We do testing strictly in-house; any minor problems with effectiveness and safety - I can fix quickly. I'm *very confident* with my work, you know my capabilities. The components are relatively cheap, as will be production. We're talking a net profit margin close to *three hundred per cent*!"

"But," interrupted McNeil, *"that's illegal*!"

"True," confirmed Winstone. "Nothing this profitable comes without risk. But you know who my father is. *Senator* Benedict Winstone. For the last twenty years. Need I say more?"

"You think he'll be on board?" Asked McNeil. "That's the only way I would consider this."

"Absolutely. I guarantee it. My neck is as much at risk - maybe more - as your own."

"What's your plan?" Asked the C.E.O.

"My Dad's chief-of-staff is having a birthday party for his daughter's 21st this coming Saturday. Small gathering, maybe twenty guests and I've been invited. My plan is to ask Allison to be my date. She will have the 'honor' of being the first test subject. Unfortunately, she'll never be aware of her new status."

Allison McKenna is Delta Pharma's chief accountant, reporting directly to the C.F.O. She has been with the company since the beginning and is very good at her job. She is very pretty with a great personality. At 5 foot, 10 inches she was nearly as tall as Brick. Her vivid blue eyes stood out in stark contrast to her black hair. Brick had been smitten from the moment he had met her. She liked Brick and they had already been out on several dates, but he sensed she lacked any sexual interest in him. Perfect subject, he reasoned; *two birds with one stone.*

"I'll slip the powder form of the pill into her drink and go from there. Worse case scenario, she won't suspect *date rape* because she trusts me, and I've never come on to her. Depending on what happens, we'll expand the scope of the trial from there. Let the *Pandora Project* begin!"

"Okay…I guess," consented McNeil. "Be very careful. You know what's at stake."

"Absolutely," confirmed Winstone, "It will be a *pleasure.* You'll be first to see the report."

****. **. ****

They quickly made their way up the long path to the house, anxious to get out of the wind and the 16-degree air. January in New Hampshire. Brick glanced up at the huge two-story colonial style home. He'd been here a few times with his Dad, each time awed by the exquisite detail of the building. This was no "McMansion."

At the door, they were greeted by a young lady who took their coats and scarves. "Welcome," she said, smiling. "Enjoy your evening." Brick glanced around the room, quickly spotting the six-foot Bandy Tylor. Statuesque; athletically trim with smallish breasts, long perfect legs and a beautiful face. She got her looks from her mother. The signature red hair was her Dad's contribution. *Jesus, I'd love to get her in bed,* floated through his mind.

Brick headed toward her, Allison in tow. "Hello, Bandy," he said, "Happy Birthday! Happy *21st* Birthday!"

"Thanks, Brick…thank you for coming. It's good to see you again - been awhile."

"It has," he replied. "I wouldn't miss this for the world. Oh…let me introduce my friend, Allison McKenna."

Bandy reached over to shake hands with Allison, "A pleasure to meet you," she said, then pointing to her left, "the bars over there; don't mean to be rude, but I've got more greeting to do. We'll definitely chat later," she said with a friendly smile.

"Of course," replied Brick. "Talk to you later. Again, *Happy Birthday*!" They went over to the currently vacant bar and ordered their drinks. Brick spotted an unoccupied loveseat adjacent to a coffee table, suggesting they "set up shop" there; Allison agreeing. She said she needed to "freshen up," Brick nodding in acknowledgement as she left in search of a guest bathroom.

Perfect! Thought Brick; gleefully rubbing his hands together. He reached into his pocket, retrieving a mini-zip lock packet containing a white powdery substance which he discreetly emptied into Allison's drink. *All right,* he thought, *the Clock begins now for tracking the evening's events.* Grinning, he softly said aloud, "The things I do for Delta Pharma."

Allison returned, sitting next to Brick. They began sipping their drinks while they watched the newly arriving guests, commenting on their dress, venturing guesses about their occupations, neither of them as yet recognizing anyone. Finally, several couples arrived who they were acquainted with. Allison drained her glass; Brick glanced at his watch, noting it was now 9:00 P.M. He suggested they get up and start mingling with the other guests. For the next hour, they chatted with this one and that one. Brick suggested they refresh their drinks, then sit for a spell - maybe do some people watching.

After about twenty minutes of commenting about various guests, Allison's tone suddenly took a more *randy* bent.

"Look at that blonde," said Allison, "the one with that skinny guy. Those are store-bought tits if I ever saw any." Giggling, she continued, "Got nice legs, though."

"Hold on a second," interrupted Brick. "I agree with your observation - but shouldn't you be checking out the *guys*?" He said with a sly smile.

"You know, you're right," acknowledged Allison; reaching over she began to gently rub Brick's thigh, coming tantalizingly close to his crotch.

"I don't know what's going on, but I'm starting to feel *really horny*."

"So?" Interjected Brick. "That's a *bad* thing?"

"No, no…not at all," replied Allison. "It's just, I don't know, I've never felt this way before - this aroused. And I've never felt so…*uninhibited*."

"You do seem pretty - what's the word - *excited*," understated Brick.

"Ya think?" She whispered hoarsely, now actually rubbing his crotch. "Then again, I'm not the one with the boner."

"Okay," she said softly, leaning in toward Brick's ear. "I just want to fuck."

"Works for me," said Brick, "Let's get outta here." He glanced at his watch. 10:40 P.M.

They politely said their goodbyes, retrieved their coats and dashed through the now 12 degrees cold to their pre-warmed car, where the attendant waited by the door, doing a quick open and shut as the pair reached the vehicle. When they arrived at Allison's house, Brick turned toward Allison asking, "Are you sure about this?"

"Does a bear shit in the woods? I think if I don't get laid soon, my head's gonna explode!"

****. **. ****

Benedict Winstone stepped out of the expansive Master Bathroom into his equally expansive Master Bedroom. He saw his wife, Judith, wearing a flimsy, transparent negligee, lying on their massive bed. She is looking up at him with just a hint of a smile. *Still beautiful after all these years,* crossed his mind. *Her generous breasts nice and firm, still-flat tummy, and those long, sleek legs.* He felt himself growing harder. He went over to her, dropping his robe before sliding in beside her. He quickly unfastened the string holding the negligee together, briefly cupping her breasts before sliding his hands down each side of her body. Benedict straddled her, parting her thighs with his knees. As he tried to insert his cock into her, she softly yelped in pain.

"What's wrong, darling?" He asked. "You're really dry."

"I know, Ben, sorry," she responded. "I think menopause is finally beginning to set in. Would you hand me the Vaseline?" He handed her the tube, allowing her time to apply the lube to her dry vagina.

He pushed his still hard member into her and began thrusting. In little more than two minutes he was spent, suddenly pulling out of her. He leaned over, kissing her softly, but firmly. "I love you just as much as ever."

"I know you do, Ben…and I love you. Always will." She slid off the bed and headed into the bathroom to use the bidet before returning to their bed. She climbed in next to her now fast asleep husband. *I DO love you, Ben,* she thought, *but you don't excite me anymore like you used to. I don't know what to do.* She fell asleep, waking about an hour later, startled to discover two fingers inside her now very wet pussy. She slowly pulled them out, brushing over her erect clit. She paused a beat before rubbing what Ben liked to call her "little love bump" - in a slow, circular motion until she orgasmed - struggling mightily to remain quiet.

. **.** **

Brick followed Allison to her bedroom. She asked him to stand by the door and just watch. Which he did. She reached behind her back, located the zipper, pulling it quickly down, allowing her dress to drop to the floor; unhooked her bra, allowing it to likewise o drop. Brick stood there, mesmerized by her smallish, firm breasts - accentuated by very hard nipples, definitely *outsized* compared with her breasts. Glancing down, he noted a dense bush behind the pantyhose. He walked over, roughly pushing her down on the bed. She laid there, breathing heavily as he literally ripped her pantyhose off, casting them aside. He used his hands to part her thighs; dark pubic hair surrounded her labia, the lips slowly continuing to part on their own, exposing the damp opening, her erect clit bulging out at the top of the cleft.

He dropped to his knees, simultaneously pulling her to the edge of the bed. He took her clit in his mouth, gently sucking, then flicking it back and forth with his tongue. He pulled the lips further apart, thrusting his tongue into her vaginal opening. Moaning loudly, she grabbed his head with both hands, pulling him in closely as she ground her pussy against his mouth. After he was sure she had cum a few times; he pulled away, stood up, and in a blink stripped off all his clothes.

"Oh My God!" Exclaimed Allison, for the first time seeing what had to be at least a nine-inch cock - and *really thick* in the bargain. She immediately took him into her mouth; enthusiastically working him, saliva dripping from both sides of her mouth. He suddenly pulled it out before he ejaculated prematurely. He pushed her down on the bed; as she spread her legs wide, he plunged his throbbing cock into her, varying his strokes - fast…then tantalizingly slow.

For the next thirty minutes, they fucked their brains out; changing from missionary to doggy, to her on top - finally culminating in missionary. Able to hold on no longer, he pulled out; semen landing on her pussy, belly, tits…even reaching her chin.

They quietly laid side by side; him in awe of the power of his *Pandora* - wondering where *all that* had come from. She had never had such intense orgasms in all her life.

Chapter Two

McNeil read aloud from the Report in front of him, "...he pulled his cock out of her tight, wet pussy, spraying cum all over her belly. He rolled to the side, exhausted by his monumental effort to do the impossible - satisfy the insatiable woman."

He slid the report folder across the desk, Brick catching it just before sliding off the edge.

"Jesus Christ, Brick!" He exclaimed. "This is pornography - plain and simple."

Brick pushed his chair away from the CEO's desk, laughing uncontrollably. Regaining his composure, he slipped the offending document into his briefcase then pulled out a different folder. He stood, handing it to McNeil as he smoothed his tie with his other hand. The CEO began reading the new document as Brick sat back down, stifling a round of oncoming giggles.

"Sorry about that, Chief. I just couldn't resist. The look on your face was worth a million bucks!"

McNeil waved a hand in the air dismissively as he continued scanning the report. He put the folder down, looking across at Winstone. "It's not that I don't have a sense of humor, Brick, but you need to understand just how serious this stuff is. If something like that ever got out..."

"It's headed straight to the Shredder, Chief, promise," assured Brick. "And I do appreciate how important this thing is. I'll be more…*formal* going forward."

"Good. Obviously, the current formulation is effective insofar as the *arousal* aspect. What about *duration?* Did you notice any mood swings? How was her demeanor the following morning?"

"Nothing of note, at least so far. We were both pretty exhausted and fell asleep after cleaning up. The next morning, she seemed fine, and I left after breakfast. She said she would be spending the day with her friend, Sue, and that she would see me back at Delta on Monday. We've been friends awhile and have dated a few times, though this was the first time with - if you'll pardon the expression - a *happy ending.* I'm assigning a couple of my most trusted staff to discreetly monitor her for at least the rest of the week."

"All right," said McNeil, standing up. "I think we're off to a very promising start. We know the current formulation is effective, but we need a broader sampling. There's bound to be side-effects, no matter how minor. Keep me posted."

"I'm on it," assured Brick. "Well, back to the salt mines, but I'm still a little sore," he joked.

"Poor you," said McNeil dismissively.

****.**.****

When Brick arrived back at his office, he saw Deborah Prout and Molly Skye sitting in the Reception area. These two were among the most trusted of his research staff. Both were very bright and exceptionally discreet, making them his top picks to monitor Allison McKenna for the coming week.

They both knew her - Deb had actually socialized with her - hopefully would be able to gain her trust in a short period of time. Both had read the report (in clinical terminology) describing his encounter with her two days ago but had no idea he was her male partner. He invited them into his office, where he explained what he needed them to do. Both women seemed eager to begin this unique, highly sensitive assignment. Molly asked if she could remain for a moment; Deborah got up and left the room.

Molly Skye possessed an outgoing, charismatic personality; well liked by all who knew her. She had one serious personal problem, however. She had virtually no sex drive, in spite of *really* wanting to experience sex on all levels. Though not attractive - "plain looking" would be the polite term - because of her great personality Molly should be able to have a normal, if not vigorous, sex life. But her libido was flat. She proposed that she be included in the study, pointing out her ability to be relatively objective in self-reporting - an advantage of her considerable experience as a researcher.

Brick pondered her offer, quickly concluding she was an excellent candidate. "I agree Molly. This is definitely a 'win-win' situation. I need you to complete the Study Questionnaire and we'll get started right away. Do you have any preferences as to sexual pairing?"

"Thank you so much Mr. Winstone! I have no partner preferences as to race or gender, though I would prefer my initial encounter be with a male. I'm ready to begin whenever you want."

"Wonderful, Molly. We'll get started today. I already have the perfect partner in mind. Go to the lab and complete the necessary paperwork. Oh, you'll need a physical exam. After that, you'll be ready for your initial dose. I'll arrange your encounter."

Molly again thanked him profusely as she walked toward the door. After she left, he picked up his phone and called his best friend, Ted Dixon. "Hey Ted, how you doin'? Listen, I've got a proposition I think you're gonna like…"

**. **. **

Ted disconnected the call, sat back in his recliner, and began reviewing what his friend had just told him. He still couldn't believe his good fortune. Brick had explained that one of his female researchers had requested to be part of his "aphrodisiac" drug study. Brick was wondering if perhaps his friend, Ted, would be willing to have sex with the girl - in the name of science, of course. *Are you shitting me??* He thought. *This is Great! I haven't got laid in over two weeks.*

When Brick described her; kind of plain, nicely styled brown hair, average height, pretty legs, *great personality* - that jarred his memory. He remembered meeting her briefly at the research lab; she had a great sense of humor, a really cool person. He had immediately taken a liking to her. *Molly* something….*Skye,* that's it - *Skye. She* had made a joke about her name and something about the sun and moon. Anyway, he remembered really liking her. And now I'm gonna get to have sex with her - *and it's all her idea*!

Tonight, 7:00 P.M. at Cassidy's Place steakhouse in Merrimack. Gonna be cold - the weather guy said it was dropping below zero tonight - guess we'll have to find a way to stay warm, was his final thought before heading in for a nice long shower and the opportunity to deal with his unruly boner.

**. **. **

Hearing the door to the garage open and shut, Robyn yelled, "Is that you, Sean?"

"Who the hell is Sean? I'm the filthy, dirty neighborhood rapist - and I'm here to have my way with you!" Sean Wilder was the Chief Investigator for the Hillsboro District Attorney's Office in Manchester. Standing six feet even with sandy hair, emerald green eyes, and movie star looks, he turned female heads heads everywhere he went. Unfortunately, he had dropped out of circulation a little less than ten years ago, having wed one Robyn Torino, now *Wilder*.

Appearance-wise, they were a match made in heaven. On the tall side at 5'11" she had dark brown hair, chestnut brown eyes, and - like her husband - movie star good looks. She worked as a private investigator, but only part time. Robyn had a great professional reputation, putting her in high demand; but was finicky about the cases she accepted and worked only when she got bored. When she did work, she put all her focus and energy toward her client's needs.

"Well, Mr. Rapist, get your ass down here and show me what you got."

A moment later, Sean came into the Den, where he found Robyn in *his* recliner, watching the Australian Open tennis tournament on their new 72" UHD OLED TV, a Christmas present to themselves. "Jesus, it's cold out there. The thermometer shows six degrees above zero."

"Yeah, I know," she replied disdainfully. Robyn had been born and raised in Orlando and was a Florida girl through and through. Admittedly, she enjoyed the six weeks of the brief New England summer; she had elicited a wedding day promise from Steve that they would resettle to Florida in twenty years, if not sooner. He knew she was dead serious. Robyn hated the cold and bitched incessantly from January to April.

"Well, get ready to go back into it," said her husband. "We're meeting Tom and Kris at *Cassidy's Place* for dinner tonight."

"Damn, you're right, I almost forgot. It's Kris' 41st." She glanced at her watch, displaying 4:45 P.M. "Well, no time for boom-boom, Mr. Rapist; not if you want to be there at the appointed time. Put your gun back in its holster. Maybe later…if you're good," she teased.

"I will," he said, "don't want to go off *half-cocked.*" They both laughed.

Robyn got up and headed to the stairs leading up to their bedroom. "Give me about half an hour honey."

Sean sat in his now vacant chair, intent on catching up with the current match.

**. **. **

2016 Canal Street, Apartment 22 read the bronze address plate. *This is the place,* thought Ted as he pressed the doorbell. Within seconds, the door opened, Molly smiling broadly as she gestured for him to come inside. As soon as he stepped in, she quickly shut the door.

"God it's cold out there - gotta be below zero," he said.

"You're right," she confirmed. "The weather guy said it's eight below and may drop another ten degrees before morning. Coldest in twenty years. *Global Warming My Ass*."

Ted laughed at the off-hand remark, thinking, *this is gonna be a great night.* She was dressed in light brown corduroy slacks and a royal blue knit sweater. The calfskin boots added two inches to her 5'8" height. She had perfect teeth and nicely styled thick, naturally wavy hair. Overall, not bad at all. He felt proud to have her for his date. She grabbed a heavy coat, and they headed out the door toward his waiting Lexus SUV.

** ** **

Tom slid Kris' chair in before taking his own seat opposite Sean. Tom Clipper is a cardiologist resident at Manchester Medical Center. He is a 5'9" man with average looks. Slightly overweight at 195 pounds, he nevertheless carries it well.

His *significant other* - the birthday girl - Kris Wood is a psychiatrist whose practice is located in the Medical Park, part of the Manchester Medical Center. Today is her 41st birthday. Kris is a 5'9" blonde, blue-eyed beauty, looking more like 31. She and Tom have been a couple for almost ten years.

Before that, Kris and Sean had been together for nearly a year. After their break-up, she became involved with Tom. Later, she introduced her friend from Florida, Robyn, to Sean. They quickly fell in love, getting married after a brief engagement. This situation never posed any problem for Kris and the foursome have remained close friends all this time.

"Thank you for celebrating my birthday with us," announced Kris.

"Our privilege and pleasure," said Robyn, raising her glass. All four clinked glasses in a toast.

"Don't forget next month," said Sean, "we do it all over again for Robyn's 40th."

**. **. **

The Matre'd escorted Ted and Molly to the cozy booth in the corner he had reserved earlier.

After sitting - side by side - Ted glanced around the dining room to see if anyone familiar was about.

Suddenly Molly said, "Oh look! The table straight across from us - in the middle - are those the movie stars in town?" (There was a movie being shot on location just north of Manchester).

"No, no," answered Ted, laughing. "That's Sean and Robyn Wilder - he's with the D.A.s office and she's a private investigator. I don't know the other couple, but she's gorgeous."

"Well, they *could* be movie stars, they're really good looking."

"Agreed," said Ted. "But looks aren't everything - just look at me."

"You're fine-looking, *I'm* the plain one…"

"…No, that's not true," protested Ted.

"Wait, Ted. I know how I look. I'm *Plain* looking. Not ugly, not beautiful - just *plain.* It's Okay, I'm cool with who I am. How a person looks is largely a matter of genetics. All you can do is work with what you've got. It's who the person *Is* that matters. That's what's important. "

"You know, Molly, I couldn't agree more," he said, reaching over, placing his hand over hers. Just then the waiter arrived to take their orders. As the waiter left, Ted noticed some kind of commotion going on at the bar. Very unusual… Cassidy's was known for its quiet elegance.

. **.** **

A very drunk Brick reached over, lightly touching the arm of the middle-aged woman sitting on the stool next to him. "You know you've got really nice breasts. My mother's got really nice breasts…"

She quickly pulled her arm away as her husband stood up, walking over to confront Brick, now tottering on his stool.

"You've got one chance to *walk* out of here. Leave. Now." Said the 6'4" man towering over him.

"DO YOU KNOW WHO THE FUCK I AM??" Shouted the severely impaired Brick. In what seemed an instant, the bartender, himself a very large man; was standing in front of Brick. He grabbed him by the arm, quickly dragging Brick - yelling a string of obscenities - around the bar and out the back door. The bartender returned, apologizing profusely to the couple; offering them a free bar tab for the remainder of the evening along with a prime table and anything they cared to order.

As Brick was being escorted out the back, Molly asked, "Who was that? Did you recognize him?"

"No," replied Ted, "I couldn't get a good look at him. Just some drunk. I've never seen anything like that before - and I come here a lot."

Over at Kris' table, she also asked, "Who was THAT?"

"That," explained Sean, "was Brick Winstone. His father - you may have heard of him - is Benedict Winstone, a New Hampshire Senator for the past twenty years. Brick's brilliant. Also, an asshole. When I was a Manchester P.D. police lieutenant, I had several encounters with him. His Dad got him off every time. Talk about 'above the law.' That's what you can do with money and power."

"What's he do for a living?" Asked Kris.

"I don't know exactly," replied Sean, "but he works for Delta Pharma. I understand his father has quite a financial stake in the company. So, big surprise. Although he is a certified Mensa."

Chapter Three

The waiter set the bowl - containing a humongous brownie with two generous scoops of ice cream, topped off with whipped cream - between them, handing two spoons to Ted. Digging into the dessert, Ted remarked, "It's been a long time since I've enjoyed a date this much Molly!"

"Likewise, Ted. But before we get to the "fun" part, let me be transparent with you. I'm sure Brick explained the clinical part of it, but I want to assure you that *I really like you* and I'm looking forward to *finally* having a great sexual experience. I really want to have a good sex life, but my screwed-up body chemistry has prevented that. I've always had the desire for intimacy, just couldn't translate it into physical feelings. Speaking of which - I'm beginning to feel real tingly down there; I think the pill is starting to kick in."

Surprised by her candor, he exclaimed, "Let's go girl! We've got a job to do!" They dropped their spoons and pushed away from the table and the half-eaten dessert. Ted dropped a generous tip on the table before they made haste to the cloak room.

**. **. **

The Uber driver helped Brick over to his sofa, then turned and left, quickly closing the door behind him; the living room temperature probably dropped ten degrees during the brief moment it was open. Brick plopped down on the sofa. Suddenly remembering the older lady with the great tits at the bar, he unzipped his fly, pulled out his cock and began stroking the limp member, unable to get even the hint of an erection before passing out on the sofa.

****. **. ****

Robyn lay naked on the bed, looking at her husband's slightly curved cock in all of its erect glory. Sean walked over; she immediately took him in her mouth, swirling her tongue around the head before suddenly engulfing the entire length of it.

"Oh, God!" He exclaimed, pulling out before he came. He glanced at her hard nipples, begging to be suckled. He began alternating between the left and right; his right hand reaching down into the waiting damp. She slowly parted her legs as he plunged first one finger, then another into her thoroughly wet cunt, eliciting soft moans. He slowly withdrew the invading digits, moving upward toward the crest of her pubic mound, along the way finding the *bump* that was slowly swelling, pushing its way through the thick bush; her clit finally poking thru the forest of fur.

She grabbed his member, prompting him to push toward his prize, but she placed her other hand on his groin, bringing his advance to an abrupt halt. He immediately understood her intent as she moved his cock's head back and forth over her now engorged clit, grunting and groaning in ecstasy; finally releasing her grip as she reached orgasm. Sean then plunged his cock into the depths. He felt her vagina clench and unclench as he increased the tempo of his strokes before suddenly slowing down. Robyn knew what was next; she felt his throbbing penis as his semen shot into her in a series of spasms.

After a long, passionate kiss, he rolled off her; the pair lying silently for a few minutes before she got up to use the bidet.

The satiated couple quickly drifted off to deep slumber, their spent bodies needing to recharge.

** ** **

Kris returned to their bed, having just inserted a fresh tampon. "Damn, I can't believe I'm still having periods at forty-one. And on my *actual birthday*. Talk about adding insult to injury…"

"Still," interrupted Tom, one eyebrow arched, "there *are* alternatives," pointing down to his crotch.

Standing by the bed, hands now on her hips, Kris exclaimed, "Wait! *Whose birthday is it??*" They both broke out in laughter.

** ** **

Kicking the door shut behind him, Ted carried a giggling Molly down the hall until she suddenly said, "Stop - in here." He carried her over to the queen bed, gently setting her down. She stood up, ripping off her overcoat, unceremoniously tossing it in the corner, before pulling off her boots. Next, she unfastened her slacks, letting them drop to the floor. Molly grabbed the bottom of her sweater, using both hands to pull it over her head; now naked save for her panties. Ted stood; transfixed by her smallish, but perfectly shaped breasts, nicely accentuated by two dark, perky nipples.

"Don't just stand there, take your clothes off…unless you're too shy," she said.

"No problem!" Announced Ted, stripping off his coat, shoes, socks, corduroy pants, and his sweater. Just as he was about to pull down his jockey briefs, she stopped him.

"Wait! Leave those on. Come over here. Now."

He happily did as instructed. Upon reaching Molly, she pulled him in for a kiss; lips parting, inviting tongues to mix and probe. Ted was rock hard. They broke the kiss and fell back on the bed, Molly on her back, Ted on his side. He reached over, beginning to smother her with little kisses, starting at her long neck, slowly working his way to her breasts; gently biting one hard nipple, then turning his attention to the other. After a few moments, his left hand slid down to her panties, where he hesitated a moment before assuming a kneeling position in front of her.

Ted slowly parted her thighs, simultaneously running his hands up to her panties. He put the palm of his left hand between her legs, pressing on her panties, already wet from the overflow of her moist vagina. He quickly pulled her panties off, revealing a clean-shaven mound. She spread her legs wide, putting her meaty labia on display. He brought his face up to her crotch, using his fingers to part her lips further, now exposing the opening to her vagina.

Ted got busy, pushing his mouth into the dampness, using his tongue to explore her nether region. He found her clit - small, but really firm. He used his fingers to pull back the protective foreskin, exposing the petite white nub that was the clitoral head. He began swirling his tongue around the tiny object; she grabbed his hair, pushing against that wonderful tongue.

Molly shouted, "I'm Cumming, I'm Cumming! - Don't Stop!" as she writhed on the bed. Temporarily spent, she lay back on the bed. "That was Wonderful! I came at least four times!"

He stood, looking into her eyes, saying, "Do you want to have intercourse now?"

Staring at the boner straining against his underwear, she reached over, grabbed his briefs and literally ripped them off. "No. I want you to Fuck Me with that Fat Cock of yours! I want you to Fuck My Brains Out!" She shouted, not caring if the entire city heard.

And fuck they did. For the next hour and twenty minutes they did *missionary*. They did *cowgirl*. They did *reverse-cowgirl*. They did *doggy*. He fucked her on the bed. He fucked her on the floor. Finally, he fucked her on the computer desk. She came so many times she lost count. He came *three* times; not including the unplanned fourth time in the shower - *in her ass!*

Afterward, they enjoyed some wine and cheese in the kitchen. "Would you like to stay over, Ted?" She asked.

"Yes," he replied. "If you really want me to."

"I do. *I really, really* do."

"Then I guess it's settled. Gotta be honest, though. It's gonna be a while - a long while - before I can perform again, I'm kinda sore."

"No worries. I need recovery time as well. You did your job. Over and above. That was the best sexual experience I've ever had - I know, I know, *the pill.* Sure, that's a big part of it. But I like you, Ted. *I really like you.* I feel a connection beyond the sex…tell me if I'm overstepping my bounds - I'm a big girl, I can take it."

"You're not overstepping, *I feel exactly the same way.* He reached over the table, kissing her.

**. **. **

Brick held his throbbing head with both hands. *How the hell long does it take for four extra-strength Tylenol to kick in,* he wondered. *Gotta get a handle on this binge drinking,* he chided himself. *Christ, I can't remember how I got home last night.*

He pulled his cellphone out and saw the message from Ted: "Had a great time last night with Molly. Matter of fact ended up staying over at her place. I'm sure she'll give you all the details in her report, but from my *lay* point of view (no pun intended) everything exceeded my expectations. Plus, *I really like her.* Thanks for the assignment. If I can be of further assistance…"

All of a sudden, the office door opened; his secretary, Dana Brice, came in, flipping on the office lights.

"TURN THAT GODDAMN LIGHT OFF!!" He yelled.

She quickly switched the light back off. "Sorry, Mr. Winstone, I didn't know you were in here."

"So, *What Is It,* Dana?" The irritation evident in his tone.

"Miss Skye asked me to leave this on your desk," handing him a sealed manila envelope.

He took the envelope from her and offered an apology, "Sorry I yelled at you, Dana. Had a really rough night."

"That's Okay, Mr. Winstone," she replied before turning around, beating a hasty retreat out of there. Now, he began to feel even worse about snapping at Dana. He liked her, plus she was kinda cute. She had nice legs and really great tits. Glancing at the manilla envelope on his desk, he realized there were more important matters at hand.

Using a letter opener, he ripped open the envelope and pulled out Molly's *Brief* of the previous evening's encounter, using the typical anonymous approach, written entirely in clinical terms.

> *Female Subject #1 (hereafter referred to as S1) ingested the 2.5 mg pill form of the test drug code named*: Aphrodisiac *at 7:50 P.M.*

> *She reported sexual arousal - specifically, a general "tingling" sensation in her genitals. S1 informed Male Subject #1 (hereafter referred to as S2) of her rapidly increasing level of arousal.*

> *8:25 P.M.*
> *She reported an urgent desire for her breasts and genitalia to be masturbated. S2 began by massaging her erect nipples before focusing on her pubic area.*

> *He commenced masturbating her; specifically, inserting two fingers into her thoroughly lubricated vagina, then shifting to massaging the inner lips before digitally stroking her now fully erect clitoris. He reported retracting the clitoral foreskin, exposing the glans, which he began gently licking.*

> *At this point, S1 reported she was engulfed by an intense series of orgasmic pulses originating with the clitoris; causing her to pull his head into her crotch;*

thereby maximizing the effect of his mouth and tongue on her external genitalia.

Subsequent to her orally inspired multiple orgasms he inserted his fully erect penis into her well-lubricated vagina, wet to the point that the excess vaginal lubricant was running down one leg.

They began having intercourse in the so-called "missionary" position, continuing through a variety of positions to include woman facing forward, woman facing back, standing rear entry, sitting front entry, and woman superior. This session concluded at 9:55 P.M.

S1 reported losing her count of orgasms; S2 reported three orgasms during this period. It should be noted that at 10:45 P.M., the subjects engaged in spontaneous anal sex while together in the shower.

S1 reported the experience to be at once exciting and satisfying with a post-coital sense of overall well-being.

This subject has been diagnosed with severely deficient levels of progesterone and testosterone. An addendum to this report documenting S1 hormonal levels for a one-week period will be submitted at the end of the time frame.

Brick slipped the Report into his briefcase, grabbed his overcoat and headed into the reception area where he paused at Dana's desk. "I'm headed over to the lab, then Mr. McNeil's office. I'll be back later this afternoon." Smiling, he continued, "Again, I'm very sorry for my behavior earlier. It was very rude. I assure you it won't happen again."

"Thank you, Mr. Winstone," she replied, returning his smile, "Think no more of it."

**. **. **

Brick was greeted at the door of his father's home by the butler. "Good afternoon, Sir. How may I help you?"

"Good afternoon, Roland. Please tell my mother I'd like to see her."

"Certainly, Sir." He turned and headed up the grand staircase. He returned a moment later informing Brick; "Madame will see you in her sitting room, Sir." He thanked the butler and headed directly to her sitting room; actually, a living room-sized area furnished with a large sofa, two loveseats, and a padded antique chair that dated back to colonial times. Upon his entrance, his mother rose from the aforementioned chair.

Recently turned 54, she didn't look a day over 40. Her nicely styled short hair had numerous streaks of grey running throughout. A handsome face with hardly a wrinkle; a perky little nose that her husband loved to tease her about, and her eyes - an unusual smokey shade of grey he had yet to see on another person. A tall woman with the figure of a thirty-something, she always stood out among her peers. And those breasts…

He immediately banished that last thought, replaced with *why couldn't I have inherited more of HER genes?*

"Come over darling, give your mother a hug." He stepped over and they briefly embraced. "To what do I owe the pleasure?" She inquired as she took her seat, simultaneously indicating he sit in the loveseat directly across from her.

"Well, Mom, I don't know if you're aware, but it's Matt McNeil's 60th birthday on Thursday. Endora (his wife) wants to have a surprise party for him, but as luck would have it, their home renovations won't be completed in time. I was wondering if I could offer our house as a stand- in? There'd be twenty-five to thirty guests."

"I did not know this will be his 60th. Of course you can have the party here. Unfortunately, your father won't be able to attend, he's going to be in Geneva for the next five days for that big economic conference."

"Thanks, Mom. I'm sorry Dad will miss it – they're such great friends."

"That's the nature of his job. I'm sure they'll have a 'just the two of them' celebration when he gets back in town."

After about thirty minutes of chit-chat about the family, Brick took his leave. He had to swing by the lab and then to McNeil's office to discuss the project, along with some other unrelated company matters before returning to his office for what he hoped would be a little change-of-pace.

Chapter Four

Dana quickly ran through the emails, deleting the junk and filing the rest in the "Active - Unread" folder. She reminded herself to inform Winstone about the call from Molly Skye, advising her she would be gone at least two days to attend to her ill mother.

Dana Bryce was an attractive woman who was fond of men, preferring their company to those of her own sex. She really didn't have any girlfriends - with the exception of Sue Alvarez. Sue had gone out of her way to help Dana get settled in her new job. They soon realized they had very compatible personalities, quickly becoming friends and confidantes. She also liked Molly, but then *everybody* liked Molly. She was one of those rare individuals that got along with everyone. Besides being naturally charismatic, she never had a bad word to say about anyone.

Her thoughts returned to the opposite sex. She *really* did enjoy male company. She wasn't naive; male lustfulness was a given. Not usually a problem for her; she very much enjoyed sex.

That said, she didn't have a very good history when it came to long term relationships. Her latest affair with her previous boss ended with their break-up and her leaving the job; his promise to leave his wife and marry her going south. *When will I ever learn?* she scolded herself for the umpteenth time.

Then her newest boss, Brick Winstone, came to mind. Until this morning, he had always been pleasant to her. *Still, everyone's human...this is probably just a one-off. Overall,*

I like him, even though he's not particularly good looking. But certainly not ugly. Kind of like Molly Skye, just "plain" looking. Which is kinda surprising. His Dad - the Senator - is really handsome and his Mom is a beautiful woman. Guess he didn't luck-out in the genetic department.

She glanced at her watch: 3:50 P.M., ten minutes to quitting time. Just then, the door opened; Brick stepping in, a *Starbucks* bag in hand.

** ** **

Endora sat at her desk, looking at the invitation list displayed on the computer screen. Twenty-six people total, mostly company friends with a smattering of others, notably David Wozniak, the current District Attorney of Hillsboro County. Dave and Matt had been friends since college. Which brought to mind his other best friend, Ben Winstone, New Hampshire's current senior Senator and one of the most powerful men in Washington. Unfortunately, he wouldn't be at the party. After one final review, she sent a copy to Brick for his perusal.

God bless Brick Winstone and his Mom, ran thru her mind. Endora would be forever grateful for them hosting Matt's surprise 60th birthday party at their beautiful home. She got up just as the incessant hammering and sawing noise came to an abrupt halt. It must be quitting time. Indeed, her watch displayed 5:00 P.M.

** ** **

Reaching into the bag, Brick pulled out two large cappuccinos', followed by a super-sized blueberry muffin. "Sorry I'm late. The Starbucks store was smacked. Will you stay just a little longer. A little peace offering to say I'm sorry. Still feel bad about my rude behavior this morning."

"Sure, Mr. Winstone. Can't have you feeling bad. Not to mention wasting a perfectly good Starbucks cappuccino," she said, a smile beginning to emerge.

"Great!" Taking an exaggerated look at his watch, he asked, "We're off the clock, so please call me Brick, Dana…may I call you *Dana?*"

"Yes, you may, Mr....er, *Brick,*" she said, obviously feeling awkward in the moment. She glanced at him, forcing a smile as she took a long sip of her cappuccino; unaware it had been spiked with the powder version of his experimental aphrodisiac.

He chatted her up about her previous job: how she liked this job, the people, the working environs - encouraging her to be candid. She said she was quite pleased so far; pointing out how Sue had gone out of her way to make her feel comfortable, while Molly made her feel welcome.

Brick said everybody liked Molly; in his opinion she was the "glue" in the company's social fabric. He expressed some surprise, however, about Sue's role. Brick said she was a great worker - efficient and dependable but at the same time had a reputation for being a loner. Nonetheless, he was happy to hear how caring she had been for Dana. For the next forty minutes they continued discussing the history of the company and its growing influence in the local economy.

Dana was slowly beginning to feel aroused. As she looked at Brick, she began to see him in an entirely different light. And growing more aroused by the minute. Suddenly, Brick - who was watching her intently, said in an off-handed manner, "You know, I skipped lunch today. I need to get something to eat, but I'm not fond of eating alone. Listen, if you don't have any plans, would you like to join me for dinner? I know a nice place overlooking the Merrimack River. It's not far from here and the food is great. My treat. What do you say?"

"Sure," she replied, "sounds good to me. Thanks for the invite." She stood up and grabbed her coat; Brick doing likewise. As they headed to the parking garage, Brick suggested she could follow him to the restaurant, saving them a trip back to the office garage; Dana readily agreeing.

During the short drive to *The Pilgrim* restaurant, Brick felt pleased with how well his plan was working out. He knew his *Pandora* drug was beginning to take affect; the tell-tale signs beginning to emerge - the slightly glassy eyes accenting the "cat's eye" pupils, the emerging facial flush, and the continuous subtle shifting from side to side in response to the building genitalia tension. He would have to help her stay under control through dinner without her realizing he had any idea what was going on with her.

Dana followed Brick's Lincoln Navigator at a safe distance. She was feeling good, maybe even a little euphoric - like she felt after taking a Percocet. She was certainly feeling horny. *Really horny.* The six-week sex drought since her break-up was apparently catching up with her. She had no doubt she would be pleasuring herself tonight. She was feeling all tingly between her legs. Dana reached down and touched her very wet panties. Suddenly worried she had started her period, she pulled her hand back up, expecting to see blood covered fingers. She was relieved to see the wetness was a clear, vicious fluid...her vagina was just lubricating.

Brick turned into the main entrance of *The Pilgrim,* pulling into the Valet's station; Dana right behind him. He got out, telling the attendant to take care of both his car and her BMW.

He motioned for Dana to get out, which she did, then walked over to join him.

As the waiter escorted them to the table by a window, she glanced around. *Yeah, it is a nice place, but there isn't gonna be much 'looking out the window,' it's almost dark. Wouldn't be dark yet back home* (Dana was a native of Cocoa Beach, Florida). After they were seated, the waiter handed them menus, promising to return shortly for their drink orders.

"So, what do you think?" Asked Brick.

"It's really nice. Now I'm getting hungry." She flashed a smile, thinking, *he's looking better and better...maybe I'm gonna need more than a little hand action tonight.* She continued looking at Brick in silence - couldn't stop thinking about sex, when a thought occurred to her, *I know, I'll do the leg-squeeze thing.* In high school, there was a boy in her chemistry class she had a crush on. Sometimes he got her sexual imagination really worked up. She learned - by accident - that tightening and un-tightening her thighs brought her to orgasm. And this was before she learned all about masturbating. *I'll give it a try,* she thought.

Across the table, Brick had noticed her watching him, when her expression suddenly changed, and her breathing grew stronger. She blinked her eyes a few times and made a low, grunting sound. He was about to ask her if she was all right when the waiter arrived to take their orders.

Dana looked over the menu. "Hmmm, what would you recommend, Brick?"

"Do you like Italian?" He inquired. She nodded in affirmation. "I think the veal parmigiana would be an excellent choice," he suggested. Again, she nodded, this time with a smile.

"Two veal parms with Caesar salads," he ordered. Glancing up at Dana he asked, "I'm having a glass of the house Chardonnay, would you care to join me?"

"Please," she replied.

Glancing up at the waiter, He said, "And two glasses of Chardonnay as well."

"Very good, Sir," he said as he collected the menus. "I'll be back momentarily with your beverage," then turned to go.

After the waiter took his leave, Brick reached across the table, laid his hand atop Dana's and asked, "Are you feeling all right, you look a bit flushed."

"I feel fine," she said, smiling broadly. "More than fine...I feel great. I'm having a really good time - just hungry - and that's your fault!" She said with a laugh. Dana's little "squeeze" trick had worked. She'd had a pretty intense orgasm bringing about a substantial reduction of sexual tension, though - truth be told - she was still pretty damned horny.

The waiter returned with two large goblets of chardonnay. A few minutes later they were both pleasantly surprised by the earlier-than-expected arrival of their meals. Over dinner they had an impromptu getting-to-know you conversation. He said he was born and raised in Manchester, living there all his life except for when he lived on campus at Harvard for a few years. Dana in turn described her upbringing in Cocoa Beach where she was born; then going to college at the University of Florida, where she majored in Biology before switching to computer science.

Over dessert, they discovered that neither of them was in a relationship; in Dana's case, without going into details, said she was over her last relationship and ready to move on. She didn't want another serious relationship for the foreseeable future but was open to dating - alluding to satisfying her "needs" as a young, healthy woman. Once again, she felt the sexual urges building up, overcoming whatever inhibitions she still had left.

She looked Brick in the eye, saying, "Thank you for dinner, I've had a wonderful time. I hope I'm not being too forward…would you like to come by my place after we leave? I have an apartment in Hooksett. If you don't, that's Okay, I understand - springing it on you like this."

"No, No!" Exclaimed Brick. "That would be wonderful. I'm ready to go." *She's ready,* he thought. *This new drug is gonna change a lot of things - most especially, yours Truely's sex life.*

They waited outside barely a minute before their vehicles arrived. He tipped the attendant, then pulled out, Dana right behind. Once on the highway, he pulled over, allowing Dana to pass so she could lead the way to her place. Fifteen minutes later, she stopped in front of a series of townhouses, hers being the third of seven. She motioned for him to follow, pulling her car into the driveway. After the garage door opened, she pulled her car in, while he parked the Lincoln in the driveway. He got out of the car and walked into the garage as she hit the wall remote to close the door. He followed her through the entry into her house.

Brick stopped for a moment, looking around. He noted a larger-than-expected living room adjacent to a small dining area that included a kitchenette with a refrigerator, oven, microwave and dishwasher. Everything was new, including a leather sofa, loveseat, and recliner. *"Very nice"* he observed.

"Thanks, I really like it. Sue helped me get this place. I'm sub-leasing for the moment. Want to see the *piece de' resistance?"* She led him down a short hallway opening into her bedroom. As soon as they were inside, she pulled him in close for a kiss, which quickly turned into an exploration of tongues. She felt his growing erection pressing against her. She pushed him back, then unzipped her dress, letting it drop. Next, she deftly unhooked her bra, tossing it to the side. He stared at her nicely shaped breasts, standing firm, nicely tipped with two twin peaks. Finally, she slipped off her panties before sitting on the edge of the bed. "Your turn," she announced.

In just over a minute, he was standing buck naked before her, his cock standing at attention.

That Thing's Gotta Be Ten Inches, she marveled. "Come over here," she ordered, taking him into her mouth. He groaned in pleasure as she alternately sucked and licked him, dividing her attention between the head and the long, thick shaft to which it was attached. After a couple minutes of that, he pushed her back and she laid flat on the bed.

With his hands, he pushed her legs apart, revealing a clean-shaven pubic mound above her pink slit, the inner lips already parted. He dove right in, tongue darting in and out of her wet cunt before retreating upward to attend to her engorged clit. She moaned in ecstasy, cumming over and over. She pushed his head away from her crotch. "Okay," she said hoarsely, "time to fuck!"

She drew her knees back as he climbed on the bed. He plunged his member into her wide-open love tunnel; quick strokes, slow stokes, long strokes, short strokes. He felt the vaginal walls grip his cock in a tight embrace. He pulled out, rolling her over to fuck doggy-style for a while before deferring to her whims. Dana rubbed her clit for a bit before climbing on for a ride, finishing him by raising her hips and positioning her ass slightly to the rear; the tip of his cock just barely at the entrance, maximizing the friction on her clit. She controlled the stroking, masterfully bringing them to a simultaneous orgasm, with his cock squirting semen onto her ass, labia, and inner thighs. She reached down, using her fingers to prolong the orgasmic sensations as long as possible. Finally, they collapsed on the bed both exhausted and satisfied. After a few minutes lying together, Brick got up and began to get dressed.

"I've got to go. Have a breakfast meeting with the CEO before work. I had a wonderful time. I'd like to maybe do this again sometime - no pressure, let's see how things work out. I know I can count on your discretion. Work is work and this is…well, *this.*"

"No worries, Brick. I'm a big girl. And *discretion* is my middle name. I'd love to have a re-do, if and when the time is right. You certainly know your way around a bedroom!"

"Wonderful," he replied, "likewise concerning your bedroom comment. See you at the office."

Dana got up, giving Brick an affectionate peck on the cheek as he prepared to leave. "See Ya."

"Goodnight, Dana. Thanks for a really great time," Brick said on his way out the door.

**. **. **

Brick finished his call to Ted and disconnected. He had left *The Derby* after having breakfast with Matthew. That was twenty minutes ago - he was now less than ten minutes from the mansion where he would be meeting with his mother. He had successfully convinced Matthew to come, along with Endora, to a gathering at his mother's house tomorrow night celebrating her "friend's birthday." He was pleased with how all the pieces of his plan were falling into place. True, Ted wasn't crazy about his role - his "ethics" standard catching Brick by surprise - but he finally caved in. *He'll get over it,* thought Brick. Ted would be bringing Allison McKenna while he would bring Sue Alvarez. He knew that wouldn't be a problem for the smitten Ted, since Molly was out of town and Sue Alvarez is a well-known lesbian.

A few minutes later, he turned the Lincoln into the private drive to the mansion.

**. **. **

Ted set his phone down on the table. He wasn't happy. He knew from his long-time friendship with Brick that he was prone to pushing boundaries about most anything. But what he was now proposing was downright unethical. Even in the name of *Science.* He had explained about tomorrow night's surprise birthday party for Matthew McNeil; how he would be bringing Allison McKenna and Ted would be bringing Sue Alvarez. Ted knew Sue was a hard-core lesbian so that would eliminate any potential problems for him and Molly. Everything was cool up to that point. But then things went off the rails.

Brick wanted Ted to help him slip the powdered form of his experimental drug - the one he called *Pandora* - into the women's drinks. That wasn't right. Not ethical. They should give consent. But he was adamant. According to Brick, that part of the study had to be conducted surreptitiously if the study results were to be accurate. True, Molly had - and probably would continue to - benefit from this drug. But these were regular women - sure, one was a lesbian - but they didn't need to be "fixed." Brick pushed hard, calling in all favors he felt he was owed over the course of their lifelong friendship. Ted finally caved. Ethically, he owed that to his friend. Still, he was very unhappy.

**. **. **

Brick sat across from his obviously distressed Mom who had just finished telling him about last night's intruder caught looking in various rooms. One of their security team chased him, but he got away before the police arrived. Brick finally got his mother calmed down. He suggested they temporarily add two more security people which seemed to momentarily allay her fear.

Chapter Five

Brick pulled up to the front entrance, setting the shifter to Park. Attendants on either side of the Lincoln opened the doors: Brick and Allison exiting the front seats followed by Ted and Sue emerging from the rear. They escorted their dates to the large entry where they were formally greeted by the butler. After checking their coats, the party entered the main parlor just in time to see Judith Winstone, Brick's mother, come down the main staircase. She was dazzling in a classic black evening gown, specially designed for the occasion. Brick was still amazed at how beautiful his mother looked at 54. Apparently, this was a widely shared view, as every man present turned to watch her slow, gracious descent down the stairs.

Brick's little entourage discreetly waited by the foyer while the other guests were greeted by his mother. Once she was alone, they walked over.

"Mother," he said, "you look absolutely beautiful. Allow me to introduce my guests; you already know Ted; this is his companion, Sue Alvarez. And I believe you previously met Allison McKenna, Matt's Senior Accountant at Delta Pharma."

Judith acknowledged Brick's guests, shaking hands with each in turn.

"And where is the guest of honor?" Inquired Brick.

"Oh, he won't be arriving for at least another hour. His wife, Endora, is bringing him here under false pretenses," confided Judith. "He thinks he's coming to a surprise birthday party for one of my friends. If things go according to plan, he won't know it's for *him* until the cake is brought out."

"How clever," observed Sue. "What a great idea."

"Indeed," replied Judith, nodding in Brick's direction. Sue and Allison clapped briefly as a smiling Brick took an exaggerated bow.

Over the next twenty minutes, the rest of the guests arrived, including David Wozniak, the current D.A. for Hillsboro County, and Robert Landry, the Senator's longtime friend and Press Secretary. Recently divorced, Ben told him to take some time off and stay behind in the States. When Judith told Ben about the party, he suggested she invite Landry to be a sort of *de facto* representative for him. Judith - who was very fond of Bob - thought that was a great idea. When she contacted him, he eagerly accepted; confiding he was now ready to once again begin socializing.

David Wozniak was the Senator's best friend. They had known each other since grade school. Winstone had helped him get his job, tipping the scale; Wozniak's rival was equally popular and actually had more experience as a prosecutor. Moreover, Wozniak was a good friend of the guest of honor. The three of them had been thick as thieves for many years.

Brick watched as his mother received Dave Wozniak and his wife, Sarah. After chatting for a few minutes, they left to mingle with the other guests. Next Landry stepped over; his mother greeting him with a hug and kiss on the cheek. It was then that Brick noticed the sudden change in his mother's demeanor. As the pair talked, she couldn't take her eyes off him; she was continually touching him on the elbow and arm. After apparently hearing something amusing, she threw her head back, laughing heartily before playfully touching his chest, then gently pushing him away - laughing all the while. He seemed especially attentive toward her; by Brick's reckoning - fawning all over her as they continued their animated conversation. Suddenly he was jarred from his fixation…

"…Brick, *BRICK,*" said Allison, tugging on his sleeve. "Earth calling Brick Winstone!"

"Whaat…," mumbled a confused Brick, glancing at Allison.

"I said, *Look at Bandy, she has her tongue so far down Jim Rafferty's throat, she's gonna suffocate him!*"

Turning his head toward their table, he said, "Oh…oh yeah!" And began laughing, the rest of the group joining in. Brick, still looking in their direction, said - just loud enough for the pair to hear, "Jeez, get a room you guys." They looked back at Brick's table, laughing nervously.

"Damn, Brick," observed Ted, *"that was pretty cold."*

"They'll get over it," replied Brick, smirking.

Sue stood up, "I gotta powder my nose."

"Me too," said Allison. The pair left the table. "Be back in a few."

Now alone, Brick took the opportunity to set his plan in motion. He surreptitiously added the powdered drug to each of the ladies' drinks, telling Ted, "In about an hour, I want you to slip this (he handed a miniature baggie to Ted) into Bandy's drink. About an hour. The timing's crucial."

"Jesus, Brick."

"Just do it," admonished Brick.

The women returned to the table in time to see Matthew McNeil and his wife, Endora arrive; Judith walking over to greet them. Brick noted Landry hanging back. He had been with his mother- like *joined at the hip* - ever since he had arrived. *Okay, Mom,* thought Brick. *Since you obviously like this guy, I'm gonna - how do they say - "hook you up."*

What had a moment ago been a rudimentary thought now came into full focus. Earlier today, he had the security tech set up surveillance cameras outside her bedroom window. After the tech left, he hung back, strategically placing four state-of-the-art, CIA quality tiny cameras with audio capability about the room. They were virtually invisible; it would take a specialized "bug" scanner to reveal their existence. His initial motivation was to keep an eye on his mother's safety. That now changed. He was going to ensure that Mr. Landry *Would Not* be a threat to his parents' marriage. Part Two of his emerging scheme involved spiking his mother's drink with his aphrodisiac drug, *Pandora, ensuring* she would lose all inhibition, turning her fantasy into reality. *I know - underhanded;* he admitted to himself - *but it's for the greater good.*

About thirty minutes after the McNeil's arrived, Judith had everyone gather round. A pair of servers wheeled out a cart topped with an enormous birthday cake. Judith's friend, playing the part of the "birthday girl" stood on one side of the host, while the McNeil's were on the other. The servers went right by the decoy, passed in front of Judith, and stopped in front of Matt McNeil.

"*SURPRISE!!!*" Yelled all the assembled guests in unison, a flabbergasted Matt standing silently. As everybody whooped and clapped, Brick seized the moment, stealthily moving to the side table with his mother's wine glass. He quickly emptied the contents of the packet into her wine. Confident he had not been detected, he nonchalantly returned to the main gathering. During the next hour, the guests went up to Matt individually and in groups, wishing him a happy birthday and in some cases, to present him with gifts. After getting over the initial shock, Matt appeared to be thoroughly enjoying the party, happy for all the love and respect coming his way.

While all this was going on, Brick was paying attention to certain individuals. He (and Ted) was amused by how Allison and Sue were acting. They caught the women "making eyes" at one another and playing "footsie" under the table. Ted had successfully spiked Bandy's drink about 45 minutes ago and now she was all over Jim - at least as much as she felt she could get away with - under the table rubbing his crotch with her shoeless foot. Things continued to slowly, but steadily escalate.

Brick was especially focused on his mother, who in turn was the subject of special attention from one Robert Landry. Yet everything was still under control, even though various activities were beginning to push the boundaries of normalcy. All of that was about to change.

It was creeping up on 10:30 P.M. The guest of honor and Endora thanked Judith for a wonderful time, allowing that they were no longer the *party animals* of yore and needed to get their "beauty rest." Judith said she understood and gave

Matt an affectionate peck on the cheek before they turned to go. Thus began the exodus of the older crowd. In quick succession, pretty much everyone over 40 took their leave. The remaining guests included Bandy Tylor, her date, Jim Rafferty; Brick and Allison; Ted and Sue; *and* Robert Landry - Judith Winstone's apparent paramour for the evening. Judith summoned their butler, Roland.

"Roland, I want you to dismiss all the staff for the remainder of the night. Please thank them for their excellent service this evening. There will be a substantial bonus for everyone in the next salary check, including yourself. Before you retire to your cottage, please ensure the house is secure."

Thinking, *This Is Most Unusual,* Roland bowed, saying, "As you wish, Madame," then turned to carry out her instructions.

Brick and Ted sat quietly at their table, amused by the smoldering looks the women were exchanging. *Now the real fun begins,* crossed Brick's mind. He had told Ted that they would excuse themselves for the evening; telling Allison and Sue they both had to be up early for work the next day. He would tell the women they could remain longer if they wished - he already knew how that would go - and they could charge their Uber rides home to him. He and Ted would go their separate ways, presumably home in Ted's case. He watched his mother stop by Bandy's table and chat briefly with the couple before coming over to his table.

"Brick, if you folks would like to stay, please feel free. You have the run of the house," she said with a wink. Brick smiled and nodded, noticing how flushed his mother looked. *The drug is really kicking in now,* he thought. As his mother left, he turned to Allison, telling her he was leaving; Ted quickly excused himself as well. Brick told the women to enjoy themselves.

** ** **

Judith stood at the foot of the staircase, surveying the entire *great room.* Brick and Ted were heading out the front door; Bandy and Jim were holding hands across the table, Allison and Sue doing likewise. *Holding hands?? Whatever works,* she thought. As she watched Bob approach, she realized that she had never felt so aroused - *so goddamned horny* - in her entire life. And no inhibitions whatsoever; her usual cultured persona - gone. She was breathing heavy just watching that hunk of a man, Bob Landry approaching.

When he arrived, she grabbed his hand, stretching up to whisper in his ear, "Want to come upstairs…" before she finished the sentence, she was already leading him up the staircase.

** ** **

Sue watched, fascinated, as Judith and the guy she'd been hanging with all evening went up the stairs, hand in hand. "Look at that," she said, prompting Allison to swivel her head around.

"No shit!" Exclaimed Allison. "The old lady is gonna get laid!"

"I hope I look half that good when I get to be her age," allowed Sue, matter-of-factly.

"Fair point," agreed Allison. "I know a lot of guys our age who would love to fuck her."

"You know I'm gay, right?" Asked Sue. "Anyway, I'm horny as hell. I know you like guys, but I get the feeling you might be open for a little change-of-pace."

"Well, hell yes. Follow me." She grabbed Sue by the hand and led her down a long hallway. About halfway down, she opened the door to a large bedroom featuring a king-sized bed. She tugged Sue in, pushing the door closed with her foot.

****. **. ****

"Jesus, Jim," said Bandy, "I'm really worked up. I just want to have sex…NOW!"

"Works for me!" Quickly agreed Jim. "Let's get outta here!"

"No. No time for that, I wanna fuck NOW! HERE! Come with me." She grabbed his hand, leading him down the hallway Allison and Sue had just disappeared into. She opened the door of the first room they came to. They were greeted by the sight of two naked women embracing in front of the bed.

"SORRY!" Said Bandy, quickly pulling the door shut. They continued down the hall. She stopped at the next door, tentatively turning the knob before slowly opening it. "All clear," she whispered, pulling her lover in behind her. They quickly undressed, tossing their clothes wherever. Bandy looked at Jim's well-defined, 6'4" body. His cock standing at attention. She was fixated on his fully erect cock. *All four inches of it!* It was the smallest penis she had ever seen. She didn't know whether she should laugh or cry. *Laugh* won out - *but no* - she couldn't do that. She bit her tongue, working hard to keep a neutral expression.

Jim let his eyes roam over Bandy's sexy body. Small, but firm tits…and no bush, really cool - he thought a smooth pussy was especially sexy. As they continued to look one another over, they heard their very vocal neighbor's activity next door. Bandy, listening to the lovemaking, began to feel her arousal returning. She decided to focus on anything but the size of his pecker.

"I want you to fuck me in the ass!" She suddenly decided. She turned her back to him then spread her legs wide as she bent over. She felt him poking around, his tiny cock slipping in and out of her very wet, slippery pussy (*Good,* she thought, *get it lubed up for my butt*).

She reached around, getting a tenuous hold of his little cock, finally managing to work it into her ass. Ten strokes later, she felt him begin his orgasmic spasms. Another ten strokes and he was done. One thing - he had plenty of semen. Her ass and thighs were drenched in his cum.

She went into the bathroom, grabbed a small towel and wiped her crotch and legs clean.

Returning, she saw Jim lying on his back, his now deflated cock smaller than ever. With its pink head, it looked to her like a little baby birdy in its nest. She struggled to suppress a giggle as she lay down beside him. *Who would have imagined,* she thought, looking over his tight, well-muscled athletic body - *the perfect male specimen. And I think he actually believes his cock IS NORMAL. This has gotta be God having some fun;* the thought causing her to giggle out loud.

Alarmed, Jim abruptly sat up. "*What's Wrong?*" He asked.

"Nothing, Babe. I was just thinking about my 'surprise' earlier when I opened the wrong door."

"Oh yeah. *That* was a surprise."

Just then, they heard a soft knock on the door. Bandy got up, went to the door, opening it slowly before cautiously peaking around. It was Allison, wrapped in a bath towel.

"Hey Bandy, would you guys like to come over to our room, maybe *party* a little? Sue has some killer weed."

"Sounds good. Give me a few minutes to talk to Jim."

"Okay. The door's unlocked. Just come over when you're ready."

Bandy returned to bed and told Jim about Allison's offer. He looked nervous and unsettled.

"To be honest, Bandy, I'm not too comfortable with that. Plus, I don't use marijuana. But you go ahead. I think I'm just gonna go home."

"Okay, Jim. If you're sure. I think I'll stay a little while longer. I had a really great time with you."

**. **. **

After Jim dressed and left, Bandy wrapped herself in a towel, gathered her clothes and purse, then went next door, knocking softly. After a moment, the door opened and Allison gently grabbed her arm, tugging her into the room. The air reeked with the pungent odor of marijuana.

She noticed both women also tucked under towels. Sue took a deep pull on the sizable joint she was holding then offered it to Bandy, who took a serious toke in turn. Bandy loved pot. It almost always made her horny - not that she needed any more of that just now.

While taking turns toking, Bandy related her experience with Jim and his little cock. They all broke into a marijuana-enhanced laughing fit.

"Who would have thought," tossed out Bandy, "a guy so big could be so small??" Sparking another round of boisterous laughter.

Sue abruptly changed the topic. "So, Bandy, have you ever been with a woman before?"

"Not since summer camp when I was thirteen. But I really enjoyed the experience. Actually, I learned a lot about sex that night. The girl taught me how to masturbate - fondling my clit."

"It was the first time I learned how to climax just from my clit. In my experience, most guys don't have a clue about pleasuring a girl's clit. They're either too rough or ignore it entirely."

"Well," said Allison, "you're young yet. The good news is they get way better at it as they get older - some are really accomplished, especially when in it comes to oral sex."

"So," asked Bandy matter-of-factly, "are you two lesbians?"

"I am," volunteered Sue, "Allison prefers guys, but enjoys the occasional fling with another woman - like now."

"So…as a lesbian, you don't want anything to do with men - *sexually* - is that right?" Inquired the curious girl.

"No, not all," corrected Sue. "I almost always hook up with women, but I have on occasion been attracted to certain men. I enjoy a nice *big* cock every now and again," the comment sparking another laughing fit. "Like Allison, I do enjoy the occasional change-of-pace. That said, wanna get down and dirty?" Sue stood up, removing her towel. Bandy looked her over. A nice firm body with small tits. Muscular legs with especially well-defined quads. Sue walked over to the bed and laid on her back.

Then Allison stood, dropping her towel. Bandy noted her tits were also on the small side, but larger than Sue's. *The nipples,* thought Bandy, *are exquisite. God, she could poke an eye out with those - gotta be at least an inch long!* Allison walked over to the other side of the bed, also laying on her back. Bandy, now really worked up, went over to the bed, taking the vacant middle space.

Sue spread her legs. Bandy glanced over at her smooth pubic mound. Sue reached down, using her fingers to part her pussy lips, exposing a very large clitoris. *That's the biggest clit I've ever seen - even in porn -* thought Bandy. *It's almost like a little cock.* She felt her own clit get even harder in reaction to the visual arousal.

"Do you want to touch it?" Offered Sue. Bandy glanced at her face, already flushed. She reached down, taking it between her forefinger and thumb. It did feel like a miniature cock. Bandy began a slow back and forth motion, actually jerking it off. Sue began moaning. After a few minutes, Sue shouted, "I'M CUMMING!!" Bandy glanced over at Allison, who was furiously working her fingers in the thick black bush covering her pussy.

Bandy felt her thighs being pushed apart by Sue, then two fingers penetrating into her very wet cunt where they lingered for a minute, lightly massaging the vaginal walls. Sue pulled out her fingers, then began slowly encircling Bandy's engorged clit, before suddenly moving her head between Bandy's legs, sucking her swollen pussy lips into her mouth, then using her tongue to gently stroke Bandy's clit. Bandy had a quick series of orgasms as her overflowing juices began running down the sides of Sue's mouth.

Bandy turned toward Allison and saw her thrusting a huge, 12" dildo in and out of her moist vagina as she rubbed her clit with the other hand, quickly bringing herself to a series of intense orgasms, punctuated by animal-like groans and grunts.

**. **. **

"Are you sure about this, Judy?" Bob was having some serious second thoughts. Robert Landry had been Benedict Winstone's press secretary since well, forever. From the beginning, before he was elected Senator for the first time. True, he had always had strong feelings for Judy: even before he and Sarah Jane had gone off the rails.

She had just finished explaining her "personal circumstances." Yes, she still very much loved her husband, but Ben couldn't (or wouldn't) perform sexually. And she still had her sex drive, a *strong* sex drive. She said the lack of physical relations was beginning to take a toll on her mental health. Judith knew Bob had a strong physical attraction to her. She said that this would be a win-win for both of them. She didn't want a romantic relationship; just sex with someone she was attracted to, someone she could trust. Also, she pointed out, they had been close friends for many years.

"I am sure about this," she said with conviction. "No one will ever know. Don't you want me?" She asked as she unzipped her dress and let it fall. Before he could reply, she had removed her bra and stepped out of her panties - standing before him completely naked. She sensed her nipples growing hard as she gave Bob a smoldering *Come Hither* look before moving her feet slightly apart, affording him a partial view of her full-bushed mature pussy.

That did it for Bob. Drinking her in, he grew rock hard; unable to maintain any sense of objectivity - the erect nipples at the tips of her full, but firm breasts confirming her arousal. In what seemed an instant, he was completely nude and embracing her naked body.

She felt his stiff cock press on her belly as he roughly pushed her down on the bed. She spread her legs wide, hoping he would pleasure her with his mouth before they started fucking.

He paused for a beat, looking at her full bush. She said, "I know - I'm kind of old-school." He leaned over and they kissed, entwining tongues. His mouth wandered; gently kissing her breasts, nipples, belly; finally arriving at the *good news*. He gently parted her moist pussy lips allowing his tongue to probe the dampness. She moaned softly as he arrived at her fully erect clit. He inserted a couple of fingers into her cunt so he could feel contractions as she moved through multiple orgasms; loudly grunting and groaning.

Judy gently pushed him off, then took his thick cock in her mouth, bringing him to the edge before retreating. He, in turn, rolled her over, using his legs to spread her thighs apart before plunging his cock into her, alternating between hard, then gentle, strokes. After some minutes, she rolled him over, taking the superior position, furiously stroking his rock-hard cock. They suddenly switched to doggy when, finally losing control; he ejaculated deep inside her.

** ** **

Brick was transfixed by the images rolling across his MacBook screen. For the last thirty minutes he had been watching Robert Landry perform oral sex on his 54-year-old mother before she returned the favor, spending a number of minutes with his cock in her mouth. Now, he was fucking her doggy-style; the two of them having already blown through missionary and cowgirl.

He heard both his mother's moans, groans, and grunts reach a crescendo as Landry finally came. They broke apart and began talking. He couldn't make out what they were saying - he made a mental note to fix the audio feed at the earliest opportunity. This was the evidence he needed to save his parents' marriage.

Brick went back to the beginning to watch a replay. He sat back, unzipped his pants, pulled out his hard cock and unashamedly began jerking off while he watched his mother having sex.

Chapter Six

Brick sat at his desk, mulling over the events of the previous evening. Everything had gone according to his pre-arranged plan. Except for one thing. How in the hell was he going to obtain the data he needed for the trial? He had dosed three people (four, counting his mother, but that was an entirely different situation) and it was all done surreptitiously - *not a single one of them had consented.* He thought, *What am I gonna say? "Remember the party Thursday night? Well, I spiked your drink with a dose of an experimental sex-arousal drug. I was wondering if you could complete a questionnaire about its effects for my trial study." Yeah, right. Somebody help me pull my head out of my ass!*

His thoughts shifted to his mother: *And my mother. Dear God, my Mother! What was I thinking??* He immediately began rationalizing: *It was for their marriage - I Have To Save their Marriage! It's the only way I can keep Landry away from her.* Never mind that the incident was initiated by Judith - and only because Brick drugged her. Robert Landry had been the reluctant one. He thought about the recording, watching his mother - *His Mother* - having sex, actually fucking before his eyes. And enjoying it. Like some kind of whore. And how did he respond?

Well, he pulled his cock out and started jerking off for all he was worth, splattering cum all over his MacBook. *Who Does That?* He began banging his head with his hand when he heard his office door opening.

He looked up to see Dana approach his desk. "Good morning Mr. Winstone." She hesitated, alarmed by his sweat covered face. "Are you okay Brick?" She asked as she started to walk around the corner of his desk.

He immediately raised his hand to stop her. Grabbing a couple of tissues, he wiped his brow and face. "I'm fine Dana, at least I will be once this hangover passes. Remember that Birthday party I told you about? Long story short - too much wine."

"Ah," she replied. "I hope you feel better soon. (remembering their office protocol agreement) *Mr. Winstone*. Molly Skye has returned to work and requested another dose of the trial drug. She said she's ready for the next session."

"Good. Tell her to see Sue Alvarez at the Lab. I'll send an authorizing email. Anything else?"

"No, Sir. That's it."

"Okay, then," he replied. "I've got a couple of personal errands to attend to, after which I'll be headed to the Lab. Oh, it's Friday, right? Take the afternoon off if you want."

"Thanks, *Mr. Winstone*," said Dana as she turned toward the door, "hope you feel better soon."

****.**.****

Molly set her phone down on the kitchen table, having just finished her call to Brick's office.

She told Dana she was back and needed Brick to approve another dose of the drug. Dana inquired about her Mom;

becoming disturbed when Molly told her the cancer had re-emerged.

She headed to her bedroom, looking forward to a shower before leaving for the Lab. Before she could get in the shower, her phone buzzed. She walked to the kitchen and saw it was Ted calling.

"Well, hello there! Good to hear your voice. What? No, I'm getting ready to go in. Right this minute…well actually, I'm standing here stark naked…You want me to do *what*? You're a pervert, Ted Dixon. Sure, we can meet for lunch…How about that little sandwich shop next to the Amoskeag Bank? Noon is fine…see you then." She put the phone down. Wearing a big smile, she headed back to the shower. She liked Ted. She liked him *a lot*. And not just the sex. He was a really great guy. Special.

****.**.****

Sue put her purse in the lower desk drawer, then sat down. While her computer was booting up and connecting with the Delta Pharma internal network, she thought about the previous evening's happenings, bringing a smile to her face. She felt a little residual horniness left over from last night's sexual adventures. Two newbies at the same time. *That* didn't happen everyday.

Her screen lit up; she saw a new email waiting from Brick. He authorized her to give Molly a new dose. *I really like Molly - doesn't everybody -* she thought, *kind of plain-looking, but a really nice body. I bet she'd be great in bed. Especially with this new drug. I'd like to try a dose myself. Maybe get a dose for Dana - I'd love to do her.* Sue knew she could fudge the inventory numbers; the lab had produced eighteen more doses than had been requisitioned; she was the only one aware of the error. Once she was convinced the drug was safe - well, it'll be off to the races for Sue Alvarez!

She heard a knock on her already open office door; glancing up, she saw Molly Skye standing there. Smiling, Sue said, "Hi, Molly," as she beckoned her to come in. "Bet you're here for the drug dose."

Returning her smile, Molly confirmed, "You would be correct."

Sue walked over to the Security Cabinet, looked at the retinal scan portal and hearing a click, opened the cabinet. "Powder or pill?" She asked.

"Hmmm. Powder, please," Molly decided.

"You got it." Sue reached into the powder section and grabbed a packet, then reached back, grabbing three more, which she deftly slipped into her lab coat pocket before walking over to Molly. "Here you go, girl," said Sue, "Enjoy."

"I don't know about all that, but thanks. Have yourself a great day, Sue," she said, turning to leave.

Yeah, I'd like to roll around with that one, bounced around in Sue's head as she fidgeted with the three "appropriated" packets in her pocket.

****.**.****

Brick was about ten minutes from the Mansion. He was still mulling over how he was going to resolve his study reports for McNeil, who was still under the impression that Allison McKenna had signed the study consent form (which Brick had forged). Thank God the privacy laws prevented Matt from ever discussing the study with her. And he assumed Sue Alvarez and Bandy Tylor were also voluntary participants. The only truly legitimate subject was Molly Skye.

Well, he thought, *I guess I'll just fake the reports for Allison, Sue, and Bandy. Use Molly's Report as a model. That's the ticket.* He let out an audible sigh of relief, pleased with himself for so quickly resolving the issue. He knew that he couldn't get FDA approval for the necessary wider outside trials without the required minimum of four progress reports from a minimum of four study subjects. He did a quick mental tally: *Allison, 2; Sue and Bandy, 1 apiece; and Molly, 1 - soon to be 2. Too bad he couldn't count Dana, but as a non-medical employee she didn't qualify for the Internal Trial Study.*

Turning into the Mansion drive, his thoughts quickly turned to his mother. How is she feeling physically? Mentally? Is she over-wrought from last night's experience? *Guess I'll find out soon enough.* He parked near the main entrance and walked the short distance to the front door. He was greeted by Roland who told him his mother was out on the garden veranda. Brick opened the door to the veranda; upon seeing him, his mother stood up and beckoned him over to her table.

Reaching the table, Brick bent to give his mom a kiss on the cheek before taking a seat.

"Good Morning. Would you like a coffee?" She offered. As he nodded, she picked up her cellphone to call the kitchen. "Hello, Janet. Would you bring out two coffees…some Danish pastries as well? Thank you."

He studied his mother for a moment. At first glance, she appeared to be her normal self. Then he noticed her fidgeting, hands in her lap. He quickly recognized this particular "tell" indicating she was stressing about something. "Last night's party was great. Everyone seemed to have a good time; especially Matt - your last-minute *Surprise* played out perfectly."

"Yes, dear. I was pleased as well. I just wish your father had been there." Brick sensed a touch of remorse in her tone.

"Me as well," agreed Brick, "but the circumstances were beyond our control. At least Bob made it. Sort of a stand-in for Dad." He noticed her eye twitch during his pointed remark.

"I suppose," she acknowledged just as their coffees and Danish arrived. "You *Did* enjoy the evening, right?"

"Indeed. As I said before, it was a great party, everyone had a good time, including *Moi.* I'm sorry I left early, but I had an especially early wake-up for today."

"As it turned out, the party came to an end shortly after you left. Bob stayed awhile and we chatted for a bit. After he left, I retired for the evening. Your mother's no spring chicken anymore."

"Oh, I don't know if that's entirely true," observed Brick. "Seems like there's still plenty of fire left in your furnace," he said tersely." His mother, with a quizzical expression, held his gaze for an extended moment before he looked away. She finished stirring her coffee, changing the conversation to how his father, the Senator was doing at the conference.

** ** **

Ted came through the Sandwich Shoppe door and immediately spotted Molly at a table in the rear. She stood up, waving enthusiastically. He walked over and they embraced briefly, but tightly. He whispered in her ear, "I really missed you."

"I was only gone *three* days. But yes, I missed you, too."

** ** **

Sue had been turning it over in her head for the past twenty minutes. She reached a decision. She was going to "bite the bullet" ···take the dose…see what happened. Sometimes you just gotta go for it. She already had this afternoon off - comp time for working last Saturday morning. Why not put the free time to good use? Then she made a second decision.

She picked up her phone, opened *Contacts* and made her selection. "Hi, Dana. Listen, I was wondering if you'd like to have lunch with me? I've got the afternoon off, so I can meet you whenever it's good for you…Really? That's great. Perfect…Yes, I know *The Pilgrim*. I've been there many times. See you there at One, Bye." She popped a Percocet in her mouth, thinking, *this is gonna be a perfect afternoon - what a great start to the weekend!*

** ** **

Dana set her phone down on the desk. *That worked out well,* she thought. *I was wondering what I might do this afternoon.* Dana really liked Sue, they just seemed to be really attuned to one another. She knew Sue's sexual preference - and that was Okay with her. Yeah, Dana liked men - especially for sex - but she wasn't averse to a little experimenting. Dana had only had two encounters with women - okay, three if she counted the threesome - one when she was a teenager (with a teacher, no less) and the second about five years ago. *That was a forever memory - the woman had a magical tongue.* Dana had been considering another girl-on-girl session for a while now. *Maybe this is the time* crossed her mind.

**. **. **

They walked over to the service counter and put in their lunch orders, both choosing the turkey club with creme of tomato soup. They returned to the table, just looking at one another in silence for a few moments. Ted broke the quiet, "So, your Mom's bad, huh?"

"It's not good, Ted. Listen, I don't want to dwell on that. It is what it is. They're doing all they can. Hopefully, something good will happen medical-wise. My mom won't let her situation control her life. Neither will I. Thank you for your concern, but let's put that on the back burner for now and concentrate on you and me…us. Okay?" She reached across the table placing her hand on his arm.

Ted glanced up at her, smiling. "Okay."

"So, tell me what's been going on while I was away."

His expression darkening, Ted said, "Since you asked, I gotta say I'm not too happy with the latest happenings, especially where Brick is concerned."

Their conversation was briefly interrupted by the waitress delivering their lunches.

As soon as she left, Molly prompted, "And?"

Ted detailed what he had observed at the Party: Brick pressuring him to help with spiking Sue and Allisons' drinks with *Pandora,* the same drug Molly was legitimately taking - then later doing the same to Bandy Tylor at the adjoining table. He went on to describe the changing behavior of the women, unaware they had been drugged. When Ted protested - Brick said what they were doing was for "the greater good," this of course, ringing hollow to Ted's ears. "It's like I've been blindsided by my best friend. What am I gonna do, Molly?"

Chapter Seven

The waiter took their drink orders, then handed them Lunch Menus to peruse while he was fetching their drinks. "I already know what I'm having," said Sue, setting her menu off to the side.

"And that would be…?" prompted Dana.

"The deluxe watercress salad," she replied.

"Ah, so that's the secret of your girly figure."

"That way I can afford the extra calories in our Chardonnays," explained Sue, with a sly grin.

Right on cue, the waiter returned with their wine. "Are you ladies ready to order?"

"Yes," verified Sue, "I'll have the deluxe watercress with the house bread."

He glanced at Dana, "And you madame?"

"The same," she replied, gazing at Sue, a devilish glint in her eye.

The pair made small talk about the office, lab, and recent rumors of financial difficulties when, out of the blue, Sue posed the question: "You know I'm gay, right?"

"I've heard rumors to that affect, yes," Dana said with some snark. They both laughed.

"So, how do you feel about that?" Pressed Sue.

"I think you're pretty cool. I think you're pretty sexy. I think I'd like to get to know you better. Way better. I think it would be great to be with another woman. I haven't done that in years."

It wasn't lost on Dana that her friend was becoming aroused. The flushed face. The rapid breathing. She assumed she appeared the same way to Sue.

Sue said, "I've got a proposition for you. I'm sure you're aware of Brick's new experimental sex drug - supposed to restore a normal sex drive to frigid women. He nicknamed it *Pandora*. Anyway, *Yours Truly* controls the lab's drug inventory. I just so happen to have two off-the-book doses. I'm dying to try it out. Feeling adventuresome?"

"What about safety?" Asked Dana. "You know, side effects."

"Well, I've been able to read preliminary reports," she lied. "So far - so good. I certainly wouldn't use it if I had concerns."

"Knowing the health nut you are, that's good enough for me," confirmed Dana. "Let's get on with it."

Sue glanced around furtively before pulling two small packets from her pocket, handing one to Dana. They both dumped the contents into their newly refreshed glasses of Chardonnay. After a few moments, they raised their glasses, clinking them together in toast.

Sue said, "Here's to…*A Hand In The Bush!*" They both laughed before taking generous sips.

..**.

On the drive back to her townhouse, Molly thought about what Ted had told her during lunch. She was growing more troubled by the minute. *Ted is obviously upset. Distraught would be a better word. "What am I gonna do?" he had said. More like "what are WE gonna do?"* Arriving home, she parked her car, walked to the front door and let herself in; still deep in thought when her mind shifted to a different topic. *We're getting together tonight for dinner at his place. Both figuratively and literally. And I really want to, but gotta get the physical side to kick in. So, another dose of Brick's Pandora drug before we make love. At least I'm aware of the induced stimulation, unlike the other unwitting "subjects." Brick and I are gonna need to talk.*

..**

Dana and Sue were sitting in the Mall Food Court, munching on pretzels and drinking Diet Pepsis. They had been there just over an hour, strolling around; gabbing about this and that - waiting for the drug to kick in. Then, almost simultaneously, it happened. Sue, eyes wide, looked at Dana. "Oh - My - God! I'm starting to tingle all over, especially *down there.*"

Dana, returning her friend's intense gaze, quickly noticed Sue's hardening nipples - she was sans a bra - poking out from beneath her flimsy blouse. "Jesus, Sue - *your nips!*" She exclaimed, her own breathing becoming heavy.

"I know," acknowledged Sue, with a new sense of urgency, "let's get outa here. My place. I live about a mile away, right here in Bedford." The women grabbed their purses, put on their coats, and headed for the exit, leaving their half-eaten pretzels and drinks behind. Dana followed close behind Sue and in less than five minutes they were pulling into the driveway of a modest, but well-kept ranch style home on a nicely wooded lot. She followed Sue into her home, mentally noting how it was so much warmer today - or maybe she was extra warm from her sudden arousal. Dana glanced at the open living room adjacent to a well-appointed kitchen and dining area; then it was down the hall to her bedroom, a pleasing musk scent coming from…somewhere. Both women began disrobing at the same time. Sue finished first.

Dana looked her over, focusing first on her small, but perfectly shaped breasts with exquisite dark brown nipples just begging to be suckled. She dropped her eyes, taking in Sue's legs, especially the well-defined thighs with the mound of her hairless triangle barely in view.

Likewise, Sue was checking out her now totally naked friend. *Nice tits,* she thought, her eyes drifting past the flat belly, over her smooth pubic area; slightly parted legs affording a partial view of her ample labia. *Always preferred a clean-shaven woman, better than picking pubic hairs out of my teeth.* Sue suddenly reached over, pulling Dana in close. They kissed for nearly a minute. Dana felt Sue's erect nipples press against her own breasts, her nipples growing hard in response. She felt Sue's hand between her legs; obligingly she parted them a bit more. Sue's fingers suddenly plunged into her wet pussy, then withdrew to tease her clit, rapidly growing harder.

Dana gently pushed her lover onto the bed; Sue responded by spreading her legs wide as Dana fell on top of her, then raised herself up just enough to allow her to reach her hand down between Sue's legs. Suddenly Dana exclaimed, "Holy

Shit!" And rolled off Sue, sitting up next to her. "Jesus," she said, staring at Sue's pussy, "I've never seen a clit that big! That's gotta be more than an inch long," she marveled.

"It is," confirmed Sue. As she reached down, flicking it from side to side. "Almost an inch and a half actually. *Do you like it?*"

"I think I do, *Yes, I do like it!* I've never seen anything like that before - not that I've had all that many lesbian encounters - why you could almost jerk that thing off, it's so big."

"I can…and do," said Sue. "Watch." She proceeded to grab it between her thumb and forefinger, moving the hood back and forth over its cock-like head. Fascinated, Dana watched her continue stroking when Sue suddenly yelled, "I'm cumming! I'm cumming!" Then she let go, her clit sticking almost straight up. Dana couldn't help herself. She reached down between her own legs, pushing two fingers into her wet pussy, withdrawing the now well-lubed digits to begin furiously rubbing her comparatively much smaller, but equally hard, clit: reaching orgasm almost instantly.

They both laid on their backs, side by side - done for the moment. "When I was about ten, just after my first period, I had my first clitoral erection. I quickly discovered how good it felt to masturbate. About a year later, a girlfriend and I had a sleepover. Long story short, we ended up playing with each other, but she thought my clit was a freaky thing, which really scared me. My Mom made an appointment for me with a gynecologist. He re-assured me that I was okay; in fact, said my clit was a special gift. Anyway, the pervert ended up fucking me, kinda the way you see in porn movies. It really messed with my head, the age difference and all. But I have to admit, physically it felt really, really good. So, I think that's why I prefer women - but I'm not a pure lesbian. I do enjoy a cock every now and then. Fingers, tongues - even dildos - just aren't the same. I've never told anyone this story before, but you're special, Dana, I really trust you."

Dana locked eyes with Sue. "Thanks for opening up to me. I'm touched. And I feel exactly the same about you. You're the sister I never got to have."

"Don't do the *Sister* thing!" Exclaimed Sue. "How can I have sex with my *Sister?*" They both broke out laughing. After simply holding one another for a couple of minutes, Sue swung around; both women spreading legs open; each burying her head in the other's crotch.

** ** **

Brick entered the Lab and flicked the light switch. He knew it would be vacant; two research assistants at a seminar and both Sue and Molly with the afternoon off. Now would be his best opportunity. He'd been considering this for a while. He'd done the math ten times over. If he modified the formula just slightly, and compensated for the estrogen factor, he should have a workable male version. One that would have the best effects of Viagra without requiring a repeating of timed doses. He was so confident in his research that he was now ready to become the first trial subject.

He got busy assembling the necessary ingredients, calculating the precise amount of each, then putting it all together to create the new compound. The process took less than an hour. He checked and re-checked his calculations. Satisfied he ingested the first trial dose.

** ** **

Slowly, things began to come into focus. He awoke lying on the Lab floor. His head was pounding. Sitting up, he glanced at his watch: 4:15 P.M. *Holy Shit! In forty-five minutes, security will make the first evening check. I've got to get out of here.*

Slowly, he stood up, gathering his thoughts. *Last thing I remember was drinking a glass of water with the new formula mixed in.* Holding his still throbbing head, he looked around, noticing some spilt powder on the floor. He quickly cleaned up that mess then set about returning the drug compounds to their appropriate storage bins. He took one final look around. Satisfied, everything was in its proper place, he left the Lab and headed for the parking garage.

. **.** **

Molly carried the place settings over to the table, once again admiring the vase of twelve red roses adorning the center of the table. *For me,* she thought. She was truly impressed by this wonderful symbol of special affection. *I don't know for sure, having never felt this way before...but I think I'm falling in love with Ted;* the thought bringing a smile to her face.

"Hey, Molly, come here," he said, beckoning her to the kitchen.

Dropping the placemats and silverware, she joined him. "Here, taste this," he said, proffering a ladle of sauce. She took the ladle and sampled the sauce.

Handing back the ladle, she said, *"Yum,* this is delicious! If you're asking me if the sauce is done, then, *Yes,* it's definitely ready."

"Good," he said, "because the spaghetti will be ready in a few minutes. After you finish setting the table, come back to get our salads. Then we can officially begin dinner."

On her way back to the table she thought, *And a great cook, too! How lucky am I?* At this moment, she was filled with pure joy. *If this is love, bring it on!* Molly finished setting the table, returning to the kitchen to fetch their salads.

Ted followed her back, holding two glasses of Rose', which he set at each of their places. He pulled out the chair for Molly, seating her properly. He leaned over, planting an affectionate kiss on her neck. She turned slightly, pulling him down then kissed him full on the mouth. He took his seat and picked up his wine glass, Molly mirroring him. They raised their glasses, Ted pronouncing, "Molly, I find myself loving you more with each passing day." Molly responded, "I couldn't say it any better - my feeling exactly." They clinked glasses before taking generous sips of their wine.

During dinner, they took turns describing their lives; their aspirations, their mutual desire to have children. Molly learned that Ted came from a very wealthy family, even now receiving monthly checks from his trust in excess of four figures. He confessed that he had been living a lazy life, not interested in working…basically just aimless. But he told Molly that just her presence in his life was changing all that. He had graduated from Dartmouth with a pre-med degree. Now he wanted to go to medical school and become the doctor his parents (and now he) wanted him to be. Not for Molly - well a little for Molly - *but for himself.*

Molly became overwhelmed with emotion, letting the tears flow. Ted moved his chair adjacent to Molly's and reached over, hugging her tightly. After a couple of minutes, he picked up a napkin, gently wiping away her tears. After regaining her composure, she said, "I'm sorry, Ted. I'm just so happy," with a short, halting laugh. "I love you so much."

"What about Brick?" Asked Ted,

"I don't know yet," she answered, "but not tonight, Ted, not tonight. *This is our special time.*"

They cleared the table. Ted made them each a cup of coffee and brought out the chocolate mousse he had made for dessert. They talked about a future together. Creating their own family. Then she took her pill. And they waited. To make love. Real physical love. They would become one. This time, sex wouldn't be *just sex,* but the true physical expression of their love.

Chapter Eight

7:30, Saturday morning. Daylight arriving on another cold January day; at least, *not as cold.*

He sat staring out at the street below, observing the continuous flow of people in and out of the Rexall Pharmacy just below his one room walk-up. Barely enough room for his twin bed, and a beaten-up old recliner that didn't recline anymore. Amenities (Ha!) included a small refrigerator, microwave (at least *that* was relatively new) and a decrepit toilet situated in a room no bigger than a closet. An old sink was next to the refrigerator. His most prized possession was the 19" Flatscreen he had won in a radio call-in contest. But the rent was cheap. Leaving him just enough left-over money to treat himself to the occasional meal out.

Jean LeFleur, a former Army Ranger noted for his infiltration skills was now a part time derelict, who, during his sober interludes, earned money with his superior carpentry skills. He had earned a reputation for excellent craftsmanship; finding himself in high demand for home improvement projects, especially in the upscale north side of town - where the Senator's mansion was located. He'd had quite a few gigs there. And they paid really good. But the last job - well, he viewed that as *the one that's gonna be my ticket outta here.*

He had been hired to build custom shelves and shoe racks for the Senator's wife. A major upgrade to her walk-in closet. *Walk-in closet? Jesus Christ, it's bigger - waay bigger - than the place I live in. But what a babe she is! Fifty-something, she looks more like in her thirties. God, what a lucky son of a bitch the Senator is; she probably fucks his brains out all the time. Gonna give him a heart attack. She's definitely my favorite jerk-off fantasy.*

One day near the end of the project, she came into the closet while he was working and opened the floor safe. He heard her say the combo aloud to herself as she opened it; "*47...23...17.*"

47, 23, 17. He committed that to memory. A short time after she had left, he tried the combo, slowly spinning the dial: 47-23-17. He pulled the handle. BINGO! It opened. He marveled at the wealth of jewelry inside before closing the safe's door and spinning the dial. Then the wheels in his head began turning - a plan was beginning to take shape in his mind.

The next day - the day he finished the job - he put the first step in motion. That night, he returned to the Mansion, using his infiltration skillset to enter the grounds from the wooded side. Arriving at the rear of the building, he quickly set up the ladder he had concealed in the shrubbery, climbing to the second-floor bedroom window. He had manipulated the window lock so he could open it from the outside. The light was on, but the room was empty. He lifted the window a bit - it moved with little effort. Suddenly, the bathroom door opened. She came into view, wearing only panties. He watched intently as she walked over to the bed, her breasts jiggling just a bit, then pulled on a long negligee. He was transfixed by the sight, his stiffening cock pushing against his jeans. Then the light went out, bringing his attention back to the present. He scrambled down the ladder, then concealed it behind the shrubbery before stealthily heading back whence he came; suddenly tripping over an un-retracted sprinkler head, he exclaimed, "SHIT!"

LeFleur heard someone around the corner of the house say, "Hey! Who's There?!" He immediately sprinted toward the woods and the dirt road just beyond, where his piece-of-shit, 25-year-old Ford Ranger awaited.

**. **. **

Ted rolled over to face his love. Molly sleepily opened her eyes, "What time is it?"

"It's just after eight," announced Ted; reaching over, he ran his fingers through her now disheveled, but still luxuriant, thick dark hair. He moved in closer, kissing her gently. *"It's Saturday!"* he proclaimed, "Let's *do* something."

"You mean, *like have another Go*? I'm game."

"No, I don't think I can rise to that occasion just yet. Poor *'Pepi' is pooped."* Molly laughed and laughed and laughed…Ted quickly getting caught up in her laughing jag. Last night, during their first session, Ted confided to Molly that when he was younger, one of his early partners had referred to his member as *'Pepi the Penis,'* really cracking up Molly. Anyway, they had gone on for two more sessions, lasting about an hour apiece. Ted was happy, albeit really sore.

Finally regaining her composure and now fully awake, Molly asked, "What did you have in mind? It's late January and - you need to jot this down - *Molly doesn't like the cold."*

He laughed. "Noted, but the weather has taken a turn for the better, today's high is in the *Fifties.* I was thinking, drive down to Boston, do the Museum of Science or something. Get a nice lunch somewhere. We haven't even had a real date yet and we're already engaged - well, sort of. So far, it's just been Fuck, Fuck, Fuck!" They both fell into another laughing spell.

"Okay, Babe, sounds like fun to me. Truly. But first, let me shower, then fix breakfast." Before he could object, Molly went on, "Don't say anything. *I insist.*" He threw up his hands in mock surrender.

** ** **

Brick, still pacing back and forth, looked at his watch, noting it was now two in the afternoon. He had been feeling a bit *off* ever since he got up this morning. Yeah, there were the two hour-long masturbation sessions abetted by the Porn Channel. That hadn't surprised him. Expected effects of the drug. But this other stuff…the agitation, the constant fidgeting, was really starting to get on his already frayed nerves. He went into the bathroom, opened the medicine cabinet; finding his anxiety meds, he quickly downed two capsules. After about half an hour, he began feeling a lot calmer, more like his usual self.

He picked up his phone, went to *Contacts,* and made his selection. "Hello Allison. I know it's short notice, but would you like to join me for dinner tonight?…I see…Okay, then; enjoy your evening. Another time perhaps. Bye." He was stung by the news. But how could he blame her, a dinner invitation with a two-hour notice? His thoughts suddenly took a dark turn. *She's just making up excuses. She doesn't want to fuck me. She doesn't find me attractive at all. The only reason we did it before was because of Pandora. The cold bitch.*

He went to the liquor cabinet, pulling out a bottle of *Jack Daniels.* Six shots later, he grabbed his coat and headed out the door. He'd been parked at the end of Willis Road for about five minutes watching the young blonde woman sitting in the bus stop shelter, looking around while she smoked. Then she spotted him. She leaned back, using her free hand to provocatively hike up her skirt nearly to her crotch. He started up the car and pulled around, stopping in front of her. He buzzed the passenger window down.

She stood up. "Hello, Brick; long time - no see. Got one of your magic pills for me?"

**. **. **

Ted and Molly strolled down Boston's Boylston Street hand in hand, sharing stories about each other's pasts. Ted volunteered that he had had a secret desire to play professional tennis. He was the best player on his college's Tennis Team, losing but one match in four years of varsity play. He said he could never work up the courage to express this ambition to his parents, especially his controlling father. But he knew in his heart that at best, he would only achieve mediocrity on the pro tour, whereas he had the potential to excel in the medical profession.

Molly moved close, kissing him before whispering, "Ted Dixon, you just amaze me with your insight. I think you can do most anything you want." She kissed him again. "When I was a young girl, I often fantasized about a charming and handsome young prince coming along to sweep me off my feet and make me his princess. Well, maybe sometimes dreams do come true, *My Prince*." She kissed him once more, this time with all the passion she could muster.

**. **. **

Brick woke abruptly; sitting up, he looked around his bedroom, completely disoriented. His head hurt, throbbing in waves. Glancing at the clock, he discovered it was 11:15, Sunday morning. He got up, realizing he was still dressed. Brick immediately headed for the bathroom to relieve his bloated bladder. Finishing, he felt a dampness in his underwear. Further examination revealed ubiquitous semen stains and…blood. Brick felt a wave of high anxiety pulse through his body. He stripped, walked into the shower; letting the water wash over him for at least ten minutes. He got out, toweled off, and put on clean underwear. He sat on the edge of the bed, trying desperately to recall last night's events, to no avail. The last thing he remembered was downing the sixth shot of *Jack Daniels*. After that, everything was a blank.

..**

Le Fleur looked up at Sadie, who had just finished draining the last of the cum from his rapidly shrinking cock. He really liked Sadie, even whore that she is. She sat there, wiping the corners of her mouth with the back of her hand. Her tits sagged a bit, but she *was* in her forties. He saw his cum residue on her gray-haired bush and around the edges of her pussy.

Her pussy. That was definitely her best feature. She could squeeze his cock at will and make him cum whenever she wanted. He had never been with anyone else that could do that.

She looked at him with her slightly crooked smile, asking - in her West Virginia twang - "How 'bout another roll in the hay?"

"No, Sadie," he said with a grin. "You were great as usual." He handed her three tens, then pulled another ten from his wallet. "Here girl," handing her the extra bill. "Get yourself something special."

"Why thank ya, honey," she said, taking the proffered ten. Sadie finished dressing and left.

LeFleur washed up, dressed, then headed out to have Sunday dinner at the diner down the street where he reviewed his plan for the jewelry heist, choosing Tuesday to be the night.

** ** **

Kris and Tom were in the Den watching the first women's semi-final match of the Australian Open when Kris' phone vibrated. She glanced at the screen. "Hmm, gotta take this, honey," she said. She walked out of the room so as not to disturb Tom. Kris returned in short order, rejoining her significant other. Tom asked, "Who was that on a Sunday afternoon?"

"That," Kris informed him, "was Judith Winstone."

"Wait, you mean the one married to the Senator?"

"One and the same. And she's pretty upset. Like having a panic attack. I told her to take a couple of the anxiety pills I had prescribed for her and made an appointment for nine tomorrow morning."

"She's a patient?" Asked Tom, sounding somewhat incredulous.

"Yes, I've been seeing her over a year now."

"I did not know that." said Tom.

"Why would you?" Posed Kris. "We don't usually discuss our patients with one another, at least not by name."

"You're right of course," he replied, "just kind of surprised me, Senator's wife and all."

**. **. **

Kris was sitting at her desk when the receptionist announced that Mrs. Winstone had arrived.

"Send her right in, Michelle."

As Judith Winstone came through the door, Kris indicated she have a seat in the usual recliner reserved for patients. Kris sat in her chair facing the recliner. She immediately sensed the other woman's tension.

"Good morning, Judith. As always, good to see you; present circumstances not withstanding."

Kris was quite fond of this lady, and in her professional opinion believed her to be an exceptionally strong-minded woman. Kris opened her MacBook, then asked, "So what's going on, Judith?"

"Good morning, Kris. Thank you for seeing me on such short notice."

"Of course," she replied.

"So," she began, "I've done a horrible thing, *I've betrayed Ben!*" She suddenly looked down, burying her face in her hands as she began sobbing uncontrollably.

Kris set her tablet down, rushing over to comfort the distraught woman. She hugged Judith tightly, gently rocking her back and forth. "Shhh, we're going to work this out, Judith," She whispered. Kris continued holding her. Slowly she quieted down, regaining her composure. Kris let her go, then returned to her own chair. She was very alarmed, struggling just to keep a neutral expression - this emotional breakdown was very much out of character for this particular individual. Kris' years of experience and training kicked in. She was determined to use all her knowledge and skills to help this extraordinary woman.

They sat in silence as Judith worked to regain - and maintain - emotional control. Then she began to relate what had brought her to this point. "It all started at Matt McNeil's 60th birthday party…"

Judith went on to describe her interaction with longtime friend Bob Landry - his recent divorce, her disappointment with her current romantic status with Ben. How, seemingly out-of-the-blue, she had become incredibly aroused - more than at any other time in her life. How she was singularly focused on getting an initially very reluctant Landry into her bed. She made a point to assure Kris that Bob was without blame for any of this. She had played the role of seductress to perfection. Judith described their physical encounter in considerable detail, including how many times she had climaxed…the unprecedented intensity of it all. How even the next morning, she had awoken masturbating, apparently recalling the previous evening's activities in a dream. Judith concluded by expressing great remorse. She characterized the guilt she was experiencing as more than she could bear.

Kris did her best to bring her to a calmer place; using all her psychological counseling experience to assure Judith that together they would work through this and begin the healing process. Kris was satisfied that her patient was now more settled and coping better. She prescribed some meds to help her with emotional control. Judith thanked her profusely for all the extraordinary care and support. Kris set up another appointment for the following Monday, telling Judith to call her – no matter the time - if she felt the need.

** ** **

Molly finished her Study Report and after a final review, submitted it via secure email to Brick. She was still feeling uneasy about his methodology, especially the questionable ethics. She and Ted had discussed that situation at length; both reluctantly agreeing to put it on the back burner for the time being. Her next trial dose wasn't due until Friday; the longer interlude designed to shed more light on the intensity of the drug's effect over the shorter term.

** ** **

While doing the weekly drug inventory, Sue decided to help herself to five more powder doses of Brick's sex drug. Counting the three she had already taken, ten more doses of the original eighteen remained. She knew that she would eventually take all of the remainder for her own purposes. Sue recalled what a great time she and Dana had last Friday. They had made arrangements for another session - this time at Dana's place (the place Sue had found for her) on Tuesday night. She could hardly wait.

** ** **

Brick tossed his key fob on the bar, went into the living room and plopped down on the sofa. He grabbed the Remote, turned on the TV, and selected ESPN to watch *Sports Center.* He was feeling so much better, more like his usual self. It had been a good day - a normal day at the office. Except for the arousal part. Every female he saw he mentally undressed as he fantasized about having sex with them. But that was manageable. Otherwise, the day was mostly routine. The only thing still bothering him about the past weekend was that 12 hour plus time frame he had absolutely no memory of. *Oh well,* he rationalized, *it'll come back sooner or later.* Maybe.

Chapter Nine

Molly glanced up from the Manual she was reading to see Sue holding a steaming cup of coffee out to her. As Molly took the coffee, Sue smiled. "It's Starbucks. Had to stop by the bank. Starbucks is next door, so I got a couple of cups to go and here we are."

"How cool," said Molly, returning her smile. "Thanks, Sue. Sit," indicating the chair next to her desk.

Sue sat down. "What's that?" she queried, pointing at the manual in front of Molly, "pretty *official* looking."

"Oh, it is." Molly showed Sue the title, *Pharmaceutical Testing Protocols.* "It details the polices and procedures for experimental drug testing at Delta Pharma. You know I'm a Subject in Brick's *Pandora* drug study. Anyway, I have some personal concerns about the testing methodology being employed, hence the manual. It's a starting point."

"So, you think there's something going on..."

"I'm not sure yet," interrupted Molly, "but I'm uncomfortable with some aspects of the study."

"If I can help with anything, just let me know," offered Sue.

"Thanks. Good to know. For the time being, I'd like to keep my concerns between us."

"Understood," confirmed Sue.

Sue mulled over this unexpected situation. *I had a feeling something is not quite right with Brick's study. That aside, this might be a good time to see if Molly's open to a little experimental girl-on-girl sex.* She was just about to pose the question when Molly announced, "I've got news! Ted Dixon and I are - I guess you could say - *an item.*"

"Whaat??" Exclaimed Sue. "Really? That's great Molly! I'm really happy for you guys."

"Yeah, We're going to get married. For me, this is like a fairy tale. I know it's quick. And I'm not one given to snap decisions. But this is right, *I just know it.* Ted feels the same way. You're the first to know."

Both women stood, embracing tightly. Molly returned to her desk, Sue doing likewise. Before resuming her task, Sue picked up the phone. "Hello Dana. How's everything going over there in *Brick World*? Listen, got some news for you…"

****. **. ****

Dana set her phone back down. A smile spread across her face as she thought about what Sue had just told her. *So, Molly's getting married. Good for her. And to Ted Dixon. Not my type, but he's certainly good-looking. Plus, a great personality in the bargain. I agree with Sue, they're a perfect match. I wonder if that Pandora drug had anything to do with it.*

Molly had confided to Dana and Sue that she was physically frigid, but really wanted to have a normal sex life. For her, this new drug Brick had developed to cure this particular affliction could be just the ticket. Outwardly, she wasn't showing any effects of the drug she'd now been taking for over a week. *Wait,* thought Dana, *this is the same drug me and Sue took the other day. Holy shit. If it has the same affect on her as it did for us…Jesus, Ted must be pussy-whipped! No wonder he wants to marry her. Naw…I'm sure they really love each other. At least they won't have to worry about the sex part. Looks-wise, he could do better than Molly, but she does have a great body. Plus, she's not ugly, just a "plain Jane." And she's the most genuine person I've ever known. A joy to be around.*

The office phone rang, breaking her brief reverie. It was Brick informing her he was on the way to see McNeil for their weekly meeting. *One of his best attributes,* thought Dana. *He always keeps me in the loop about what he's doing business-wise.* Unlike her previous boss.

"Okay, Mr. Winstone…So I'll see you later this afternoon…No - no messages so far…Bye."

** ** **

Brick handed McNeil the two reports from Molly along with the two from Subjects #2 and #3 (that actually he had written) then took his seat. He watched the CEO intently while he scanned the reports, judging him to be in a good mood. When McNeil finished reading, he looked over the top of his reading glasses at Brick.

Smiling, he pronounced satisfaction with the study thus far. "It appears our new drug is meeting - no exceeding - my expectations. Good work, Brick. You know, I'm tempted to get a couple of doses for Endora - you know, spice things up a little bit. Stoke the fire, if you get my drift."

"I can take care of that whenever you want, Chief…"

NcNeil quickly interrupted, "No, no, I can wait until we at least get FDA approval for the general trials."

"Sure," replied Brick, recalling (in his opinion) McNeil's over-the-top ethical standards. After another ten minutes or so of polite small talk, mostly about the birthday, Brick excused himself to resume his "busy schedule."

Brick entered the Lab facility through the rear door and was momentarily startled by Molly on her way out. They both paused a beat. "Good morning, Mr. Winstone," she said.

"Good morning, Molly," he replied. "You're looking well," he observed.

"Thank you, Sir. Have a great day," she said as she continued on her way out. *He's not looking so great,* she thought to herself, *kind of pale looking...and those dark circles under his eyes.*

Who put the bug up her ass, thought Brick, moving on to the main Lab. He was feeling a little "buzzed up" like how one gets with too much caffeine. And horny. He was definitely feeling more aroused again, without the benefit of any obvious stimulus. Speaking about stimulus, as he entered the lab - spying Sue heading toward her desk - he felt another erection coming on.

. **.** **

On the way back to his office, Brick swung into a Starbucks to pick up Lattes for he and Dana. Earlier, he had decided they should have a "love session" tonight. He was again approaching the peak of an arousal cycle, but otherwise felt quite normal - *except for the confusion...*for some reason he was getting confused over otherwise simple things: leaving his key fob in the car; at first ordering one latte instead of two; and paying for the beverages twice.

**. ** **

Dana glanced at the clock: 3:40 P.M. She was looking forward to getting home for her rendezvous with Sue. They had planned a quickie love session, then go out for dinner before returning to her place for the main event. She had taken her dose of *Pandora* about forty-five minutes ago and was already getting horny.

The door opened, revealing Brick holding a Starbucks bag. "Hello there," he said in greeting, "I've brought us a little treat."

At first, Dana was taken aback, but then thought better of it. She was in such a good mood, one of the side-effects of what she had come to regard as the *love drug*. Next, two events happened that would set the course of the entire evening.

First: Dana had already ingested a dose of *Pandora* almost an hour ago - Brick being totally unaware. *Second:* And even more significant; Brick had spiked Dana's latte with the aphrodisiac, *except he mixed up their drinks* - unwittingly consuming the drink intended for Dana. So, her behavior would meet his expectations (the result of her earlier self-dosing). He would assume his own (now greatly enhanced by the mistaken extra dose) arousal level was to be expected.

He told Dana how especially horny he felt. How he wanted to take her home and "fuck her brains out." Dana, herself super aroused, thought that was a great idea; her dirty little mind envisioning his massive cock ravishing her moist pussy.

Then reality came calling. She explained that she had previously planned a date for this evening, unashamedly describing her recent lesbian encounter with Sue. The explicit description got Brick even more worked up.

"Why can't we have a three-some?" Proposed Brick. "You already know the two of us are great together. Imagine a three-way fuck fest with a generous side of oral sex?"

Dana almost reached an orgasm just from the mental image Brick had inspired. She made her decision. *They'd have their little orgy.* She'd spring it on Sue when she arrived. Yeah, she'd probably be pissed at first with the deceit, but she'd get over it pretty quick. Sue would already be worked up from *Pandora,* just like her and Brick. And Sue had said she liked the occasional cock. Wait until she had a gander at the size of him.

****. **. ****

Dana promptly answered the doorbell, ushering Sue right in. As she took Sue's coat, her guest suddenly noticed Brick sitting on the sofa.

"What The Fuck!!" She exclaimed, mouth agape.

Dana profusely apologized for the deception, saying she understood if Sue wanted to leave immediately but asked her to stay long enough to have some wine and cheese with her and Brick. Sue stood silent for a full minute, then curiosity got the better of her. She sat on the loveseat opposite the sofa Brick occupied, her look of consternation slowly fading. As she let go of her annoyance, Sue's arousal skyrocketed. She felt things really stirring down below.

While waiting for Dana to return with the wine, she thought, *Sneaky Bitch. But the more I think about it, the more appealing it gets. I've never been with a woman and man at the same time, so there's that.*

It only took a single glass of wine to remove whatever vestiges of restraint she might have left. She looked directly at Brick. "I understand you might possess…what's the word…*exceptional equipment* - tucked away," pointing at the obvious bulge in the crotch of his pants.

He loosened his belt, unzipped the fly, and let his pants drop. As he pulled his shirt off, Dana glanced at Sue, noting her fixation on the object straining against his briefs. He pulled off his underwear, his ten-inch stiff cock bobbing a bit after being freed from its erstwhile prison.

"Holy shit," muttered Sue, obviously fascinated by both the length and girth.

"*I Told You,*" affirmed Dana.

"Come over here," ordered Sue, taking him into her mouth. He immediately began moaning as she worked him. Suddenly, without warning, semen began oozing from Sue's mouth, running down both sides of his cock. As Dana watched this spectacle unfold, she stripped off her clothes, and still standing, began to fondle herself between her slightly spread legs. Sue disengaged; Brick fell back on the loveseat, wiping his cum covered member with some tissue.

Meanwhile, Sue had disrobed. Kneeling, she buried her head between a softly moaning Dana's spread open thighs. She reached up and began tweaking Dana's stiff nipples. During all this action, Brick lay back, slowly massaging his semierect cock. He became increasingly excited as Dana began moaning loudly, grabbing a handful of Sue's hair, pulling her face in even closer. Brick thought she might suffocate her lover when Dana suddenly began bucking her hips, loudly proclaiming, "I'm cumming! I'm cumming!"

Sue pulled away with Dana moving to the side; Sue now sitting where Dana had been a moment ago. Brick watched, fascinated. He looked at her small breasts, capped by two dark nipples, which, to his delight, he saw grow stiffer by the second. Then it happened. She spread her legs wide; her labia parting slightly, exposing the pink opening to her wet vagina. But it was the sight at the top of her cunt that held him in thrall. He was looking at the biggest clitoris he had ever seen. Easily an inch and a half long, the thick shaft was topped by a foreskin she gripped between her thumb and forefinger, gently sliding it back and forth over its penis-like head.

Brick quickly moved over to her, pulling her hand away then taking the *girl-cock* in his mouth, eliciting moans, groans and grunts as he orally manipulated her erect clit. He could sense her cumming…two, three, four times. He moved his head away, rising to his knees as he prepared to mount her. Suddenly, he felt Dana against his butt. She reached around, grabbing the lower half of his cock then guiding it into Sue's wet pussy. As he began thrusting, Dana worked her hand upward to begin massaging Sue's huge clit. In a matter of minutes, Brick felt Sue cumming. He pulled out; Dana turned her attention to Brick; grabbing his cock, she began stroking him, his semen spraying everywhere: on Sue's belly, crotch and the sofa before Dana redirected his spasms in her direction. The three of them collapsed, exhausted.

"I've never seen such a big clit in all my life," observed Brick, "so sexy, so arousing!"

"And I've never seen a man cum so much!" Exclaimed Sue. "That's for sure," agreed Dana, "look, it's all over the place!" Sue began gathering her clothes, then addressed her companions. "I'm gonna go home. This has been unbelievable. Experiences like this are rare, probably once-in-a-lifetime for almost everybody…probably never-in-a lifetime for almost everybody. Anyway, it was *GREAT!* Brick, you owe Dana a great fuck. I'm gonna leave you guys to it. Dana, where's the bathroom?" Dana directed her, "down the hall, first door on your right."

After Sue cleaned up and dressed, the group exchanged good-byes, and she left. Dana and Brick remained in the living room, having cheese and wine as they talked about how she liked living in New Hampshire and how that differed with her native state of Florida - beyond the obvious contrast of climates. Eventually, their arousal levels rose once again, especially for Brick and they headed into Dana's bedroom.

**. **. **

Jean LeFleur lay in his bed, staring at the ceiling, hearing almost no traffic noises; to be expected at 12:30 in the morning. He felt both excited and anxious at the prospect of this life-changing heist. LeFleur had gone to bed, albeit fully dressed, at 8:00, a full two hours earlier than usual believing the sleep would ensure his thinking process remained sharp. Didn't quite go according to plan. He had spent most of the last four hours tossing and turning, glancing at the clock about every fifteen minutes. Now, finally, *time to go.* In exactly one hour, he would be in Judith Winstone's bedroom; there to help himself to her extensive jewelry collection; its new purpose: to finance the rest of his life.

** ** **

Judith went over to the window, raising it just a couple of inches. She liked allowing a little fresh air in. Up until a couple of days ago, that wasn't possible - the overnight temperature dropping below zero. Now however, the temps had returned to a more reasonable upper twenties. She climbed into bed, already feeling drowsy from the meds Doctor Wood had prescribed. She had complete confidence in Kris Wood. Extra-added bonus, they were really fond of one another. She knew Kris would eventually get her back on track again.

Then her thoughts turned to Bob…how selfish she had been. She felt terrible about coercing him to compromise his high ethical standards just to satisfy her lust. *THE LUST. Where the hell did that come from? I don't ever remember being that aroused in my entire life. Sure, I've always enjoyed sex - I have a healthy libido, but this was beyond the pale. I felt like a whore - and I LIKED IT. That's Okay. What's NOT okay is cheating on Ben. He doesn't deserve this. Any of this.*

That was the last conscious thought Judith Winstone would ever have.

Chapter Ten

LeFleur glanced at his watch: 1:40 A.M. He reached into his jacket pocket and retrieved the baggie containing the chloroform-soaked cloth, along with the surgical gloves he had purchased for the caper. He carefully pulled on the gloves, then retrieved the well-concealed ladder from beneath the shrubbery. After positioning the ladder, he began to climb, reaching the bedroom window in no time. LeFleur was pleased to find the window already cracked open. He carefully pushed it all the way up, then without making the slightest sound, climbed in and stood still. After a quick reconnaissance of the room, he pulled the chloroformed rag out of the baggie, positioning it so he could quickly cover the woman's mouth and nose.

Reaching the bed, he saw her lying on her back, the covers partially pulled back. Then he became confused. He didn't understand what his eyes were telling him. The exposed portion of her body was nude. He stared at her breasts for a moment, still not comprehending the scene. He looked at her face. Her eyes were wide open, but they weren't seeing anything. He touched her. Her skin felt cold. *Then reality set in.*

Oh my God, SHE'S DEAD!!! What the fuck…What the fuck! What am I gonna do??

He tried desperately to calm his panicked mind. *Well, I'm here. If I don't finish what I came for - it's on me. Shit. I don't need this. I didn't hurt the lady. I don't want a murder rap. But I'm already here. If they find out I was here, I'm so fucked. But I can't change the fact that I AM HERE. Might as well get what I came for.*

LeFleur pocketed the chloroform rag and headed into the closet, quickly locating the Safe. He began entering the combination: 47…23…17, then pressed the handle; the door opening immediately. He scooped up the entire contents, placing them in the cloth bag he had brought for just this purpose.

After a quick look around, he headed for the window; scurried down the ladder, leaving it in place as he dashed toward the woods and the road beyond, where his well concealed truck was waiting.

**. **. **

Sean had just finished shaving when his phone's ring tone went off. He glanced down and saw it was Dave Wozniak. Alarmed, he answered immediately. "HOLY SHIT!!!" Exclaimed Sean. "I'll be right there!"

Robyn, just getting out of bed, heard the anxiety in her husband's voice. "What is it, Sean? Who was that?" Sean stepped out of the bathroom, fidgeting with his tie.

"Come over here," she said. He stepped over; she began working on the knot while he talked.

"Judith Winstone is dead! Murdered in her own home. Maybe raped. Clifford Smith (Manchester P.D. chief detective) is at the scene. Wozniak wants me at the office *yesterday.*"

"Jesus Christ! Anything I can do?" Offered Robyn.

"Not yet. Wait…you should call Kris. Yesterday, Tom told me that Judith Winstone had called Kris on *a Sunday* and Kris had seen her on Monday; about what - of course I don't know. But it could be relevant."

"I'll take care of it."

Sean pulled on his suit jacket, grabbed his overcoat, and headed for the garage.

"Keep me posted," yelled Robyn, as he made a hasty exit.

** ** **

Detective Smith stood surveying the scene. Judith Winstone lay on her back, eyes open, an expression of shock frozen on her face. He pulled back the covers, revealing the rest of her naked body. Her legs were splayed open. She had been raped, no doubt of that. This sucked. Really sucked. Judith Winstone was literally "a pillar of the community." Well-liked by all who knew her. He turned to the forensic team leader waiting patiently, a rape kit in hand.

"Go ahead, Cheryl, do your thing." Smith moved out of her way and began methodically canvasing the room, looking for anything that looked out of place, anything that *shouldn't* be there. As he was making his initial inspection, one of the forensic techs motioned him over to the walk-in closet, then pointed out the overturned safe in the corner. Smith nodded, then moved to examine the safe. *So,* considered the detective, *rape, murder…and robbery. What order of events, I wonder. A planned robbery - she wakes up and he decides to rape her, then kills her OR…He comes in, intent on raping her, then after he kills her, discovers the safe and does the robbery - no, that doesn't work. The perp KNEW the combination.* His speculation was suddenly interrupted by a familiar voice.

"Hey, LeBron got a minute?" It was Sean Wilder, his predecessor as lead detective. LeBron Smith had been hired away from the New Hampshire State Police by the Chief to be the replacement for Sean, who had been poached by the District Attorney to be his Chief Investigator. Sean had mentored LeBron for about a month before assuming his new position. And Sean, in turn, had learned a lot from the seasoned detective. They have been good friends to this day.

The detective stood up, walked over, greeting Sean with a smile and his typical iron-grip handshake. "How you doing, buddy? Been a while."

"Yeah, too long," agreed Sean. "So where are we so far?"

Smith informed him that her body was discovered by the family Butler, who checked on her when she didn't respond to calls from the kitchen. She always called in her breakfast order before 7:00. At 8:00, Roland, the Butler, decided to check in on her. Discovering the body he immediately called 911. Her son, Brick was notified along with the Senator, who is on his way from Geneva.

"Brick Winstone is downstairs in the parlor. The coroner is on the way over."

Then, Smith asked him the obvious question: "So, Sean, how's this gonna go down?"

"To be honest, LeBron, I'm not quite sure. My educated guess would be Dave (Wozniak, the D.A.) will want to take lead on this, making me the Lead Investigator. Not any reflection on you. And not my choice."

"What I figured," replied Smith, "and we're cool either way my brother. What about the Feds? The victim being the Senator's wife, they're gonna want to get their nose in this."

"Maybe, but I don't think so. He and Wozniak are really tight. He's gonna want the discretion Dave can provide. Plus, Winstone trusts him implicitly. At the moment I'd be obliged if you could start the alibi interviews with family and the staff. I've got to get back to the office to help prepare for the Senator's arrival."

"No worries. I'll do the interviews while Forensics finishes up. Oh, what about the media?"

"*What about the media?*" Echoed Sean. "You're definitely the expert there, you silver-tongued fox."

"Yeah, right," laconically replied Smith. They both laughed.

**. **. **

Brick shook Dana once again, this time more forcefully. She slowly opened her eyes, "What's wrong Brick?" She asked, watching him tuck his shirt in.

"MY MOM'S DEAD!!"

Shocked, she quickly sat up, now fully alert. "What do you mean, she's dead?" Asked the thoroughly flummoxed woman.

"Dead. Like in *no longer alive!* I've got to go. I want you to call McNeil - tell him my mother's dead…I don't know the details yet. Anyway, he'll tell you what to do."

"Yes, yes, of course," she replied, "Jesus Christ," she muttered. Still trying to process all this, Dana got up just as Brick went out the door. She picked up her phone, surprised to see it was 8:40. *Shit!* She thought. *This is NOT going to be a good day.* She selected the CEO's emergency number and pressed *Call;* she reached voice mail. He already knew.

** ** **

Kris was about to head out the door when she heard her phone going off in her purse. She fished around, finally locating it. She saw it was Robyn. "Hello, girlfriend," she said cheerily, "what's up? NO!! OH GOD! OH GOD! *HOW DID SHE DIE*...Jesus." Kris collapsed onto the floor and began sobbing. "Sorry, I can't talk," Kris managed to get out between sobs, then disconnected the call.

"Kris, Kris!" Robyn yelled into the phone, quickly realizing her friend had hung up. Robyn tossed the phone into her purse, grabbed her coat and went through the door into the garage. A minute later she was backing her Lexus down the driveway, aiming to make the ten-minute drive to Kris' house even quicker.

** ** **

Molly looked across the table at Ted. Her voice trembling, she said, "That was Sue. Mrs. Winstone is dead."

"Dead?" Asked Ted incredulously. "What happened?"

"Sue said she didn't know. Just that she passed away."
"But such a young woman," observed Ted. "Looked to be in great shape...and still really pretty. Maybe in her mid forties."

"Sue said she is Fifty-four," Molly corrected. "Jesus," he acknowledged.

**** ** ****

Dana was just about to head out the door when her phone went off. It was Sue. She told Dana not to bother going in. She read the company-wide email from McNeil:

As CEO of Delta Pharma, it is my sad duty to inform you that Judith Winstone, wife of Senator Benedict Winstone and mother of Brick Winstone passed away last night. She served on the Board of Directors for this corporation. Additionally, her son, as you all know, is the Director of Research and Development at Delta Pharma.

Out of respect for the Winstone family, who are also part of the Delta Pharma family, we will be closed for business today to allow our people to grieve with the Winstone family. All employees will, of course, be paid as usual.

Matthew McNeil, President and C.E.O.

"I was thinking maybe you, me, Molly, and Allison could get together for lunch. What do you say?"

"I think that's a great idea," said Dana. "How about *The Pilgrim?* It's centrally located, and they have a great lunch menu."

"Perfect," confirmed Sue. "I'll give everybody a call, then text you back with the time."
"Great, talk to you later," said Dana before disconnecting.

**** ** ****

Kris opened the door for Robyn. Her eyes were still red, but she otherwise looked composed.

Robyn embraced her friend tightly for a few moments. The pair walked into the living room and took seats opposite one another.

"I spoke briefly with Sean. She *DID NOT* harm herself." Kris let out an audible sigh of relief. "Now, the bad part. She was murdered."

"Oh God," Kris said softly.

"It gets worse…before she was killed, she was raped."

"Goddamn it!" Yelled Kris.

Robyn got up and joined Kris on the loveseat, once again holding her. They gently rocked back and forth, Robyn whispering, "I know, I know…"

****.**.****

LeFleur sat on his bed, watching the "breaking news" on the local channel.

"…she was found dead in her bedroom earlier this morning. Detective Clifford Smith said the cause of death was suspicious, but declined to provide details, saying more information would be released later. The victim's husband, Senator Benedict Winstone, is on his way home and should be arriving later today. Her son, Brick Winstone, is at the home now. A spokesperson said he was understandably distraught and would comment at a later time. We will keep you updated as new information becomes available. For now, this is Wanda Reed; Action News Live."

He clicked the TV off and laid back. He hadn't slept a wink since getting back to his flat. Still anxious, he had nevertheless calmed considerably. His eyes closed as he finally slumbered.

Chapter Eleven

Sean said, "Thanks, LeBron, I appreciate your call. Tomorrow we really start digging in."

He climbed into the unmarked patrol car he had borrowed at the police garage for the earlier trip to the crime scene. During the drive back, he mentally reviewed what LeBron had determined so far. None of the staff were suspect at this point, most with firm alibis. Looked like the younger Winstone was in the clear as well. He stated that he had spent the entire night with his secretary, one Dana Bryce. Before he dismissed Brick, he quietly dispatched a detective to her place to get a statement. She had corroborated Brick's story - so he was out of the loop. Still, Sean had a bad feeling about this guy he just couldn't shake.

** ** **

Molly was the last to arrive. Once inside *The Pilgrim* she immediately spotted Allison, Sue, and Dana sitting at a table in the far corner. Sue waved her over. Taking the vacant chair between Sue and Allison, she apologized for being a little late, the other women brushing it off.

The waitress brought Molly a menu and asked what she'd like to drink. Molly looked around the table, noticing everybody had identical drinks in front of them.

"So, what's that?" Asked Molly, pointing at Sue's glass.

"A Long Island Iced Tea," answered Sue, quickly adding, "what we all chose."

Molly looked up at the waitress. "Far be it from me to go rogue. I'll have what their having." The waitress nodded before turning to leave. Sue shot Molly a wry smile accompanied by a *thumbs-up*.

"Hell of a way to get a day off," remarked Allison, the others nodding agreement. "Before we get too buzzed, I'd like to propose a toast to one very fine lady. She's going to be sorely missed. To Judith Winstone." The others raised their glasses, clinking together in respect.

Following a second round of Long Island Iced Teas, the waitress cleared the last of the lunch dishes. Dana said, "I could do another Iced Tea - how about you guys?" She glanced around the table.

"I'm in," said Sue. "Me too," said Allison. "We're pretty buzzed already," observed Molly, "another one will probably get us well on the way to *drunk.*" She paused a beat. "What the hell, I'm in!" The other women clapped approvingly.

After a bit more commiserating about Judith, the conversation turned to Brick and his new drug. Molly, the only known test subject, described in great detail how it affected her; the extreme arousal accompanied by all loss of inhibition. As she related her experiences, the other women began looking at one another with the dawning realization of having had the exact same experience. In the cases of Sue and Dana, they kept their experience with the stolen doses to themselves; both women quickly realizing that *before that,* they had been unwittingly drugged by Brick. Allison became especially resentful. As Molly talked, she, too, began to put *two and two* together. She stopped speaking for a moment; the rest of the table remained quiet.

"Well, *Son-Of-A-Bitch!*" She suddenly exclaimed. "He *used us. Especially you three*. For his own pleasure. I was just his cover story. *Motherfucker!*" The other women we're taken aback; while Molly was known to curse occasionally, *Motherfucker* was definitely a stretch for her.

All the women began talking at once, then Allison raised her hand. "Okay, we all agree that the prick used us. On the other hand, I've never experienced sexual pleasure at that level. *And I really enjoy having sex*. Three of us have so-called *normal* sex drives. Molly is the only one truly affected by the frigid thing, so based on what she described, the formula *works*. It does what it's intended to do. That the rest of us really like the experience - so far with no side-effects - is just a bonus, at least for us three. My point is, we've got to think this through. Do we really want to throw out the baby with the bathwater?"

"Are you saying we let Brick off the hook?" Asked Molly.

"No, No, No!" Emphatically stated Allison. "That asshole has to pay for what he's done - is doing - to us. My suggestion is we wait a bit, at least until we know more about Judith's case. We have plenty of time to figure out the Brick thing. Right now, the focus should be on the murder investigation, which doesn't need any distractions."

The other women looked around at each other before nodding in agreement. Then Allison said she was ready to call it a day. Molly suggested they get *Uber* rides home. She intended to call Ted, excusing herself while the others finished their Long Island Iced Teas. After she returned, Molly said Ted had volunteered to take everybody home, delighting the women. They all raised their glasses to toast Ted and his thoughtfulness.

** ** **

It was 3:30 in the afternoon when Senator Winstone, Bob Landry at his side, arrived at D.A. Wozniak's office. Already present were Sean Wilder, Chief Richard Daughtery, and LeBron Smith. Before the formal meeting began, each man in turn spoke with the Senator to personally express their sorrow for his loss. Everybody save Senator Winstone and Wozniak took a seat.

Wozniak reiterated the group's sorrow and pledged they would bring Judith's killer to justice, then turned the floor over to the Senator.

Senator Winstone thanked everyone for their dedication and support. He indicated he wanted the investigation to be headed by the the District Attorney in conjunction with Chief Daughtery. He emphasized he had already made it abundantly clear that this would be a *local agency* effort, with only peripheral support from the FBI Lab and its database. There would otherwise be *No* Federal presence. The President had assured Senator Winstone this would be the case. After again thanking everyone, Winstone excused himself; now needing to focus on the sad task of arranging his beloved wife's funeral.

** ** **

Tom gazed lovingly at Kris as she slept, relieved that she had finally accepted the sad reality of Judith's untimely death; more importantly, accepted that she was *Not* a factor. Now, her experience as a psychiatrist would help her to quickly resume her usual objective critical thinking. Satisfied she was emotionally recovering, he drifted off to sleep.

** ** **

Robyn was sitting up in their bed, impatiently waiting her husband's arrival. "Sean, do you think Judith knew her killer…maybe the reason she was killed after the rape?"

Sean stuck his head out the bath entry, a toothbrush in his mouth; his other hand in the air signaling he needed a moment. She heard him rinse before he came into their bedroom.

"Hadn't considered that scenario - certainly an interesting theory. Say, would you like to join the investigation? I'm sure Dave would welcome the help of another seasoned investigator."

"Well, *I am free* at the moment. Sure. I could use a little intellectual challenge. Speaking of challenges…," she moved the sheet to the side, revealing her naked body as she spread her legs apart, inviting his immediate attention. Robyn looked coyly at her husband, focusing on his crotch. She was really enjoying watching his cock grow harder, straining against its cloth prison, magnifying her own desire.

Sean tossed out an idea for a little sex-play. "Want to have a bit of extra fun?"

"I'm game, big guy. Whatcha got in mind?"

"Remember when you were a kid. Like during Halloween, bobbing for apples. Well, I've got a new variation called *bobbing for cock*. The idea is *we can't use hands - for anything*. Everything else is Okay. Like our mouths and feet."

Robyn said, "Cool, I get it. Come over here."

Sean moved to the bed's edge as Robyn positioned herself. Using her teeth, she was able to get a good hold of his brief's waistband. Sean stood still as she slowly pulled his jockey briefs out far enough to allow his hard cock to spring free. Readjusting her mouth's grip, she methodically tugged his underwear down about twenty-four inches. She stood up and used her forearms to push him backwards onto the bed. Then she climbed atop him, intentionally brushing her bushy pussy over his face before hooking the toes of her left foot into the waistband and deftly pushing the briefs down his legs until they eventually fell off.

Her next maneuver was predictable: she swung her legs around resulting in a mouthful of cock for her as his face disappeared between her legs. After allowing Sean a few minutes to demonstrate his tongue's many talents, she rolled off.

"My turn!" Pronounced her mate, positioning himself over her. Deciding to tease for a bit, he alternately penetrated her vaginal opening - no more than an inch or two - for maybe ten to fifteen strokes before plunging deep into her wet cunt, increasing the stroke speed. It wasn't long before she was moaning loudly in orgasmic ecstasy; feeling his pulsating cock as his sperm coursed into her. After separating, Sean observed, "Now *that* was fun!"

"Yes, it was," she agreed, "That's the first time in a long while I had a purely vaginal orgasm."

..**

Molly sat at the breakfast bar finishing her coffee before leaving for work. Ted came over, taking a seat on the stool opposite her. "Good morning, Beautiful," he cheerfully greeted.

"Cut that *beautiful* crap with me," she said curtly.

"Whoa, *Sorry* for saying how good you make me feel," he retorted, obviously hurt.

Molly was immediately chagrined and went over to him, hugging him tightly. "I'm so sorry Ted. I love you. I don't know where that came from. Please forgive me."

"Of course I forgive you Molly. There's not a doubt in my mind that comment has to do with that drug. A side effect. You need to put that in your next report."

She pondered his comment for a moment. "You know, I believe you're right. How insightful, Mr. Dixon. I *Will* put that in my next report. But I'm still very sorry." She leaned in for a kiss.

** ** **

Brick lay in his bed, trying to decide if he wanted to get up yet or not. *I do have a lot to do. Gotta help Dad with the arrangements.* Then his thoughts turned to his interview yesterday.

That damn black detective. Why did he have to interview ME? I'm her son for Christ's sake.

He climbed out of bed to shower and dress before meeting up with his Dad. He popped four maximum strength Tylenol to alleviate his persistent headache. Every four to five hours - or it became unbearable. Plus, he was still feeling out-of-sorts. *Something's off with me,* he thought - *still getting confused over nothing. At least the sex is good,* he reflected. *That Sue is something else with that freaky clit, but goddamn is she ever hot!* He stood still for a moment; *what am I supposed to be doing…oh yeah, meet Dad…wait, gotta shower first.*

** ** **

Sean and Robyn walked into Dave's office. Sean thought the D.A. looked troubled - beyond what was already happening. "So, is everything good with bringing Robyn on board?" Asked Sean.

"Oh - oh yeah," confirmed Wozniak, "of course. The Senator was good with it, he's well aware of Robyn's reputation. That's a 'no-brainer,' I think were his exact words."

"Good," said Sean, "you look troubled, I thought…"

"Yeah, right," interrupted Wozniak. "I am troubled. Last night a body was found off Route 101 just outside the city line. A dead hooker. Her throat was slashed. That's not all. Her genitals were mutilated. The perp ripped her all the way up to her bellybutton."

"GODDAMN IT!!" Angrily exclaimed Robyn. "We've got a real whack job on the loose!"

"Any connection to the Winstone murder?" queried Sean.

"Too early," said the D.A., "I suggest you get Smith right on it."

"Absolutely," Sean quickly agreed.

** ** **

"So," said Molly, as she accepted the drug packet for Encounter #3 from Sue, "I've got a question for you."

"Shoot," replied Sue.

Molly told her that she had a curiosity about lesbian sex - that she had been - *is* - sexually attracted to certain women. Now that she had the physical capability, she wanted to have the experience. She said she was aware of Sue's sexual preference and was wondering if perhaps she might consider having an encounter with her. "You know, *in the name of science,*" she said with a sly half-smile.

Holy Shit! Thought Sue, *this is like a fantasy come true!*

"Yes, yes, of course," she answered, the excitement evident in her voice. "But what about Ted? I wouldn't be comfortable going behind his back."

"Neither would I," agreed Molly. "I'm going to talk with him. I would be very surprised if he had a problem with it. He's very liberal-minded."

"Do you want him to join in?" Offered Sue.

"No. At least not this time. That would impact the *Study* side. I want you to know that I'm very attracted to you, which is a big bonus for me."

"And if I'm being honest, I've already fantasized about making love with you," confessed Sue.

"Sounds like a couple of women are in for a pretty good time," ventured Molly. Sue reached over, pulling Molly in for a full-on open mouth kiss. Molly stood back, pronouncing, "Well, *That's a pretty good start.* Don't mean to rush things, but I am on a tight schedule study-wise. How about tonight, say seven o'clock? You pick the place. The *Study* will pick up up the tab."

"Tonight's great," confirmed Sue, "Let's go to my place. Here's the address…"

..**

Benedict slowly recovered his composure after breaking down several times while discussing the funeral arrangements with his son. He was surprised by Brick's lack of emotional distress. *Maybe that's just his way of grieving,* he rationalized. Gordon came into the room to announce the arrival of Sean Wilder. The Senator told the butler to "show him right in."

A moment later, Sean walked in with Robyn right behind him. He walked over to the Senator; they shook hands. "Good afternoon, Sir." Gesturing toward Robyn, he continued, "allow me to introduce my wife, Robyn. She is a private investigator joining the task force."

Robyn stepped over; the Governor offering his hand. "Good afternoon, Senator. A pleasure to meet you." Sean walked over to greet the younger Winstone, with a "Sorry for your loss."

The Senator smiled at Robyn, "The pleasure is all mine. Your reputation precedes you." Robyn nodded, then went over to Brick, shaking his hand before echoing Sean's condolences.

Oh my god, thought Brick, *she's fucking beautiful,* mentally stripping her; the resulting erection straining against his slacks. Never mind it being totally inappropriate in the circumstances. He glanced over at Sean with envy, at once acknowledging and envying his good looks.

Returning his gaze to Robyn and bowing slightly he said, "Pleased to meet you, Mrs. Wilder."

As Robyn stepped back, she couldn't help but notice the huge bulge at his crotch. *Jesus Christ, he's got a boner! What the fuck is wrong with this guy?* quickly crossed her mind.

Sean glanced at Robyn, noting her odd expression. He turned toward the elder Winstone, "Would you excuse us, Senator? We need to interview Brick as part of the investigation. It's just routine. Thank you for your understanding."

**. **. **

Molly pulled into the driveway of Sue's ranch style home, just down the road from the Bedford Mall. Getting out of her car, she saw Sue waving from the side door, so she headed right over.

"No coat?" Asked Sue.

"No, it's finally warmer," said Molly, "actually, feels warmer than normal." She was correct. The ten-day cold snap was officially over, replaced with daytime highs in the low sixty's - about twenty-five degrees above normal; the area now experiencing the annual "January thaw."

Once inside, Molly pulled Sue close for an intimate kiss, Sue obligingly opened her mouth, welcoming Molly's exploring tongue. "Damn girl, I see you're ready for action. I was gonna give you a *quickie* tour of the house, then some wine before we…"

"Sure. Later," said Molly, impatiently. "Right now, I'm so fucking horny…where's the bedroom?"

It was now two hours since Molly had taken her dose. For the last hour, all she could think about was Sue; she imagined how she would look nude: her tits, those long legs and her pussy - bush or smooth…she didn't care, she just wanted to bury her face in the woman's crotch.

Sue, who until this moment, had been relatively under control; consumed with house cleaning in preparation for her company. And preparing her special homemade dip. But seeing Molly's present state - the reading on *Sue Alvarez's Personal Horny Meter* was now off the scale. She grabbed Molly's arm; unabashedly tugging her down the hall and into her bedroom.

Once in the room, she told Molly to take a seat. Then Sue pulled her T-shirt over her head, tossing it in the corner. Molly looked at her small, firm breasts, capped with dark brown nipples, already nice and stiff. Next, Sue turned around, unfastened her jeans, letting them drop; stepping out as they hit the floor. Molly admired her tight ass and her long legs, especially her well-defined thighs coming into view as she turned to face Molly; her prior question answered: a smooth pussy. Sue sat on the edge of the bed, spreading her legs wide as she laid back.

Holy Shit! Thought Molly, not believing her eyes. *That's the biggest clit I've ever seen!* Sue sat back up, gripping her clit between her thumb and forefinger, pulling back the foreskin and exposing the pink, penis-like head. Molly's own clit, a respectable size, but very small compared to Sue's unique appendage, had become fully erect.

Sue watched as Molly quickly stripped. Her breasts were nearly twins of her own, including the dark, perky nipples. Molly climbed on the bed; laying on her back, she spread her legs, revealing a smooth mound above a pussy with large, meaty lips; again, much like Sue's. Except for that clit. Molly climbed over Sue; they were now in the "69" position. Molly began sucking on Sue's out-sized clit, swirling her tongue over it, then gently nibbling on the exposed head. Molly pulled back, then stared at the stiff clit as it stuck straight up, surrounded by Sue's massive labia. Molly grabbed the mini cock between her thumb and forefingers, jerking it off. Sue arched her back as she began cumming in waves. After numerous climaxes, she rolled Molly onto her back, burying her face in the woman's wet crotch. She reached up, tweaking her erect nipples while separating the thick lips so she could force her tongue into Molly's wet cunt. They lasted about fifteen more minutes before lying still to allow their spent bodies to recover. Then they cleaned up, dressed, and headed to the kitchen to chat while they enjoyed wine, cheese, crackers, and Sue's special dip.

Chapter Twelve

On the drive over to Delta Pharma, Robyn thought about yesterday's interview with Brick Winstone. *There's something OFF with that guy - can't quite put my finger on it. Not happy he had a boner while he introduced himself. I think he knew I saw it. Weird guy. Rock-solid alibi, though. The Bryce woman verified he was with her all Tuesday night.*

The Delta Pharma campus came into view; she turned into the parking lot. *Let's see…the single-story building after the first left.* She made the turn and immediately saw a parking spot labeled *Visitor* and pulled in. Robyn entered the door marked *Lab.* The security officer asked to see her I.D. She fished her Private Investigator's license along with her Drivers License from her purse, handing them to the officer. "I'm here to see a Miss Molly Skye."

"One moment please," said the young officer; walking over to the wall phone, he never took his eyes off Robyn. After a brief conversation, he told Robyn, "All right Mrs. Wilder, go straight down the corridor and into the second door on your left."

"Thank you, Officer," said Robyn, smiling brightly. The young man nodded, returning her smile, obviously struck by this beautiful woman.

Entering the door to the Lab, she saw Molly stand up, waving her over to the desk.

"Thanks for coming to see me so quickly Detective Wilder."

"Please - call me Robyn. What have you got for me, Miss Skye?"

"And - I'm Molly," she parried. Robyn took an instant liking to this charismatic young woman, listening intently as she began her story. Molly explained her status as a subject in Brick's research study; then described her relationship with Ted Dixon, Brick's best friend. She went on to reveal what Ted had told her about Brick's covert drugging of Allison and Dana. His sole purpose - in Molly's opinion - was to sexually exploit them.

Molly continued, "I realize this has nothing to do with the Winstone case. I was hoping that - as a woman - and one with investigative skills, you might be able to help us bring this prick…excuse me, *this guy,* to justice."

"You were right the first time Molly - and *I Will* help you bring this *Prick* to justice. Tell me more about the drug." Molly went on to explain the drug's effects. That it was, in fact, very good at doing what it was designed to do. She explained in quite some detail her personal experiences. What it had done for her libido. The only side effect she was aware of was a total loss of any inhibitions. *That explains her unusual candor about such an intimate topic,* thought Robyn.

She asked Molly what she knew, if anything, about how the drug had affected both Allison and Dana. She related that both these "normal" women said that they had never enjoyed sex as much. That the intensity of their orgasms defied description. Robyn asked Molly if she thought they might be open to an interview about the topic. Molly opined that they probably would be.

"Wait a minute," she suddenly said. She got up and went across the room, returning with Sue Alvarez in tow. Molly introduced the two, then asked Sue to describe her experiences. Again, surprised by the candor, Molly's equally uninhibited friend confided that she was a lesbian before beginning her story. Afterward, Robyn asked if it might be possible for her to get a sample dose. Sue gave Molly a look, then got up and headed to the opposite side of the room. When she returned, she slid four packets of a white powdery substance over to Robyn, who nonchalantly slipped them into her purse. She quietly thanked both women for taking such a risk to help her.

As Robyn stood, Molly said, "I don't know what you intend to do with the drug samples, but the best way to understand the significance is to actually *experience* it. I can vouch for the safety aspect - loss of inhibitions aside - but I would recommend you be home if you decide to indulge."

"And," added Sue, "*this is important* - it is *Not* intended for males."

Smiling, Robyn briefly hugged the pair before turning to leave. "Thanks again."

** ** **

While Robyn was finishing up her "interview" of Molly Skye, across town at the courthouse complex her husband was being briefed by LeBron Smith concerning the murdered prostitute. As Sean examined the crime scene pictures, he was struck by the cruelty of the killer. Her throat had been slashed - she had nearly been decapitated - and her abdomen was sliced open from her vagina to her navel. In all his years of experience, he had never seen such depravity.

He set the pictures on the table. Looking over at Smith, he said, "This is one sick puppy we're dealing with here LeBron. Got to get this animal off the street before anyone else dies."

"We've got our best people on it. The newspaper already got hold of the story - they're playing it up big. The good news/bad news is it will scare the hell out of the public. We *Do* need people to be extra cautious; we *Don't* need a panic. Then again, there's the probability that this story will push the Winstone murder to the back pages."

"Maybe," replied Sean. "Remember, we're dealing with a Senator's family - and an election is coming up."

"Fair point," observed Smith. "We'll see."

Chief Daughtery entered the room with two large file folders just as Smith rose to leave.

"Chief, I've got a meeting with the Forensics Team in ten minutes. If you'll excuse me..."

"No problem, LeBron - go." As the detective took his leave, Daughtery took a seat across from Sean. "I've assigned him to head the O'Brien investigation. The Department is stretched really thin at the moment, especially Forensics. Good thing we brought Robyn on board. Speaking of which, I've signed off on the paperwork granting her full law enforcement authority until the investigation is concluded."

Seemingly on cue, Robyn came into the room. "Good morning, Chief," she cheerily greeted.

"Good morning, Robyn," he replied. "I've got the paperwork we need to make you a temporary L.E.O. Welcome to the

Manchester Police Department. Oh, before you leave, stop by the I.D. office to get a photo for your credentials."
She thanked the Chief before taking a seat next to Sean. Daughtery slid one folder over to them as he opened his duplicate. He quickly brought the pair up to date. The fingerprints of one Jean LeFleur were all over the room and closet, but *not* on the safe, which had been wiped clean. Additionally, a ladder was discovered hidden in the shrubs below the bedroom window. Moreover, castes of footprints were now available for matching purposes.

Glancing at Robyn, Sean said, "I think we need to pay a visit to this LeFleur character. Looks like our first solid lead." The detectives stood up to leave; the Chief doing likewise. After obtaining LeFleur's address, the pair headed to Sean's car.

** ** **

Brick was sitting on the sofa in the parlor awaiting his father's arrival. They had to go to the Lerner Bothers Funeral Home and make a casket selection. Which seemed pointless to him; his mother to be cremated, as per her wishes, after the church service. But Dad insisted. He wanted her buried in the family plot, like all Winstone's. Ultimately that would happen, her cremains would be placed back in the casket and buried the next day. A waste of money. A lot of money.

His thoughts turned toward the investigation. *Are they making any headway finding the killer?* He resented the Wilder's questioning yesterday. *And the married detective's thing - what? Are they going to make a TV series? I mean, I was with Dana all night. I could have brought Sue in as an additional back-up, but then I'd have to get into the whole 3-way fuck scenario. Too embarrassing. Plus, it's none of their fuckin' business. About that - I'd sure like to bang the*

Wilder woman. She kept giving me funny looks…I wonder what that was all about?

The Senator came into the room, breaking Brick's train of thought. "You ready, son?" He asked.

Brick stood up. "Ready as I'll ever be," he said glumly as he followed his father out of the room.

**. **. **

Shortly after noon, the dreaded *knock on the door* finally came. As he rose to answer, he heard a muffled "Manchester Police Department." Steeling himself, Jean LeFleur opened the door to see a beautiful woman standing next to a tall, handsome man (*these people are cops?*) even as they held up I.D.s for him to see. The man said, "I'm D.A. Investigator Wilder and this is my partner, Detective Wilder (*Jesus, this is right outta some kinda movie,* thought LeFleur).

Actually, LeFleur was feeling pretty calm, having taken a pretty potent pill for anxiety little more than an hour ago, courtesy of his *lady friend* Sadie. "Yes…?" asked Le Fleur as the pair walked right past him into the cramped apartment.

"We've got a few questions for you," began Sean. "Where were you between 11:00 P.M. Tuesday night and 4:00 A.M. Wednesday morning?"

"Right here," answered LeFleur, "watching the Celtics game. Then I went to sleep."

"Really?" Said Robyn. "Your fingerprints are all over Judith Winstone's bedroom and closet. The Judith Winstone who was murdered sometime late Tuesday or early Wednesday morning. And raped."

"I can explain the prints," offered LeFleur. "I remodeled her closet…spent the last six days workin' on it, so sure, my prints would be everywhere."

"That's your truck in the empty lot across Hanover Street, right?" Asked Sean.

"Yes," verified the man. "Why?"

"We need to search it," Replied Sean. "I've got a search warrant on the way," he lied.

Robyn had been studying LeFleur's changing expression as Sean did the *search warrant* bluff.

She looked directly at the man. "Look, Mr. LeFleur, you can really help yourself here. If you have anything to volunteer about the murder or the theft…well, that will go a very long way toward a much lighter sentence. Think it over."

LeFleur mulled it over for a couple of minutes, then blurted out, "Okay, okay! I did the robbery; I stole the jewels. *BUT I DIDN'T KILL HER!!* She was already dead when I got there!"

"How exactly were you going to pull off the robbery with her right there in the bed? The odds of her not waking up at some point are zero to none."

"I had a rag soaked in chloroform to knock her out; she was already dead, so I didn't need it."

Robyn glanced over, catching Sean's eye. He turned toward the perp. "Okay, Mr. LeFleur. We can work with that. Remember, the more you cooperate, the better your chances for leniency. Now I have to read you the standard Miranda warning."

Sean read him his rights while Robyn handcuffed him. Sean pulled out his cellphone to call Chief Daughtery. "Send over a patrol car. We have a suspect."

While Sean was speaking with the Chief, Robyn turned LeFleur around so they were face to face. "Jean LeFleur, you are under arrest for grand theft. Do you understand?"

"Yes, yes I do," affirmed the man. "Are you charging me with murder, too?"

"At this time, you are only being charged with grand theft. When we get to the station, you can contact an attorney. Tomorrow you will have a bail hearing."

They heard sirens wailing in the distance. Within minutes, a convoy of police vehicles was in front of the Rexall Drug store. LeFleur was quickly placed in a police SUV and whisked away.

**. **. **.

Chief Daugherty looked through the one-way glass, watching intently as Sean and Robyn interrogated LeFleur. So intently he was startled by a sudden tap on the shoulder. It was Cheryl Biscane, from Forensics.

"Couple of things, Chief," she said excitedly, "First, I've got to give these camera recordings to the detectives *right now.*" She showed him two time-stamped photos of LeFleur climbing into and later, out of - Judith Winstone's bedroom. "Second, you're not going to believe what we found."

"Well, first, give them the photos then we'll talk about the second part."

She went to the Interview Room door, knocked then went right in and over to Sean; without a word, handed him the manilla envelope then turned and left. He opened the envelope, briefly looking at the two photos before passing them to Robyn. "Looks like your ship is sinking pretty fast, Jean. Robyn, show him the pictures."

She held the photos up for him to see. The first was a crystal-clear image of him climbing into the bedroom window. The timestamp in the corner displayed 1:38 A.M. The second image of him climbing down the ladder showed 1:42 A.M. Now in a state of near panic, he announced, "I want a lawyer."

"I thought you might," said Robyn as they gathered their paperwork and left. Outside the Interview Room, they were met by Daughtery. He didn't look happy. "Come with me," he ordered, leading them down the hall to his office. Once inside, he indicated they take the seats opposite his desk.

"We've got a real problem here," he began,

"If it's about LeFleur's arrest…"

The Chief raised his hand to interrupt her. "No, the arrest was fine, he definitely - at the very least - did the robbery. We've got a new issue and it's a whopper!"

He revealed Forensics had identified another set of prints in Judith Winstone's bedroom. Those prints belonged to one Robert Landry, Senator Winstone's Press Secretary of some ten-plus years.

"THIS IS TURNING INTO A CLUSTER-FUCK!" Yelled the Chief, his face flushed a deep red.

Robyn and Sean glanced at each other, both sharing his frustration.

He immediately apologized. "Sorry for the outburst." They both nodded their understanding.

"I mean, tomorrow is the woman's funeral. I'm going to tell the Senator that Landry was, at the least, having sex with his wife, and at most, may have killed her. I want a 24/7 tail on him until we figure this out. For now, let's keep it among the three of us."

**. **. **

On the drive home, Robyn broke the somber silence. "LeFleur didn't kill that woman. He entered her room at 1:38 and was climbing down the ladder at 1:42. Four minutes. Before she was killed, she was raped. LeFleur raped her, then killed her, then opened the safe, emptying its contents into another container; *all in the span of four minutes?* I Don't Think So."

"Agreed," replied Sean. "As for Landry, I have serious misgivings that he's the killer."

Chapter Thirteen

Robyn finished touching up her hair. As she put the brush down, she glimpsed Sean fussing with his tie's knot. She walked over, gently pulled his hand away, adjusting the knot. "I don't understand how such a coordinated, athletic guy has such trouble knotting a tie."

"Thanks, honey. I guess we all have our *Archilles Ties* to bear," earning him a chuckle from his spouse. He glanced at his watch. "We better get a move on; we still have to pick up Tom and Kris; it's a fifteen-minute drive to the church from their house."

"You're right," said Robyn. As she walked through the bedroom, she snatched her purse off the bed, Sean right on her heels. Two minutes later, he was backing the car down the driveway. After seven more minutes, they pulled up to the curb in front of Kris' house; the couple - acutely aware of the time frame - already waiting. They climbed into the back seat, barely closing the doors before Sean pulled away.

Robyn turned to say, "A *funeral* - Jesus, what a way to begin a day."

"True," acknowledged Tom. "It is what it is, bad timing and all. But that's the morning. The rest of this Saturday belongs to us."

Kris jumped in with, "My sentiment as well. Oh, got some news. Promise this is the last work-related topic for the rest of the day."

After Kris' teasingly long pause, Robyn, gesturing with her hands said, "And…??"

"Chief Daughtery called this morning to ask if I would be a forensics consultant on that horrible rape/murder case…*And if I could 'unofficially' consult on Judith's case. Can't be official - she was a patient. As much as it hurts, I want to do whatever I can to catch her killer. Both killers.*"

"Good deal!" Exclaimed Sean. "Wait, that came out wrong, I meant it's a good deal we have you - your experience and all…"

Kris reached up; patting Sean's shoulder, "No need to apologize my friend, I know exactly what you meant. As they turned onto Pine Street, they saw a long line of cars parked on both sides of the road. The church was at least a quarter of a mile distant. Sean said, "I'll let you guys out at the church, then come back and park."

"Like hell," said Kris, "we'll walk back together." Sean parked behind the last car in line. They got out to begin the trek to the church.

****.**.****

Brick sat in the front row, right on the aisle. He was drunk, very drunk. He drank an entire fifth of Smirnoff's over the course of the night, now feeling pretty shitty. At least he wasn't getting boners anymore. So far, he had been able to conceal his intoxication - Brick had a reputation for holding his liquor well - but this was another level altogether. He glanced around to see his father moving about, talking to seemingly everybody. *Always the Senator, always the fucking politician. Never time for his wife - My Mom - so lonely. No one paid any attention to her.*

Except for Bob. Bob fucking Landry. HE PAID ATTENTION. HE FUCKED HER BRAINS OUT! He'll Get His…I'll See To That. His father returned, sitting next to him. Looking closely at Brick, he asked, "Are you all right son? You look a little pale around the gills."

"I'm fine," he said, managing to not slur his speech, "under the circumdances…um, under the circum*stances.*"

** ** **

Kris looked around as the group accepted the folded programs the ushers handed out, noting the church was nearly full. She saw a pew near the back with four open spots on the center aisle side. Robyn noticed at about the same time, quickly leading the group over. They had no sooner settled in than the organ music stopped. The minister stepped to the podium, getting the service underway with his prepared eulogy.

** ** **

Brick was staring straight ahead, then began alternating his focus. First, the coffin where his mother was sleeping. Then, the minister talking. The coffin… the minister. The coffin… the minister. *What the fuck is he talking about. He's gonna wake my mommy. Stop talking, you blithering idiot! YOU'RE GONNA WAKE MY MOMMY!!!*

As the Pastor finished his remarks, Brick suddenly stood up, then turned toward the assembly, appearing ready to speak when he suddenly fell face first to the floor.

Two Ushers, fortuitously big men, rushed up to Brick and, gently as they could, lifted him off the floor carrying him around to the back of the sanctuary and out of sight. Murmurs quickly spread through the assembly before the minister was able to bring back a sense of order. The Senator and his entourage, as subtly as they could, exited toward the sanctuary. The minister - to his great credit - was able to get the service back on track before directing the attendees toward the exits to reassemble at the cemetery for the interment.

** ** **

On the way to the cemetery, Sean, Robyn, and Tom listened as Kris offered her professional assessment of what they had just witnessed: he had simply passed out from the intense stress of the moment.

Maybe, thought Robyn. *All due respect to Kris, I think there's a lot more at play here than just grief. My intuition tells me there's something seriously amiss with this character.*

** ** **

Doctor Reston looked up at the Senator. "His vital signs are Okay, but he's otherwise unresponsive. An ambulance is on the way. They'll take him to Manchester Medical. I'll meet you there."

In the waiting room, Doctor Reston glanced up at the clock. It was almost noon. The Senator looked at him, then said, "Thank you, John. Not just at this moment, but everything you've done for the Winstone family over the years. We couldn't have a finer family physician."

The two men stood as a doctor emerged thru the E.R. door. He shook hands with the men. then said, "I'm Doctor Jankowski, the on-call E.R. Physician today. My specialty is Neurology." Looking at Winstone, he continued, "I'm afraid your son is catatonic. He most likely will regain consciousness at some point. The unanswerable question is *When.* Could be hours, days…perhaps longer. We just don't know."

"Can he be treated at home?" Asked the Senator.

"Oh yes," replied the doctor, "matter of fact - if you have the resources for the necessary medical personnel - I highly recommend it. The familiar surroundings are more conducive to recovery."

Glancing from Doctor Jankowski to Winstone, Reston said, "I'll see to it, Ben."

** ** **

Robyn clicked off the call, laying her phone on the table. "That was the Chief, wasn't it?" Queried Sean.

"It was," she confirmed. "He decided to bring Robert Landry in for questioning. Doesn't want to wait until Monday morning. Wants us to interview him now."

"Well, lets go then," said Sean. "It's 11:30 now. With any luck, we should be *off duty* and back home by 3:00." They grabbed their jackets and headed for the garage.

Chief Daughtery met them at the Main Desk. "Thanks for coming in on short notice. Hopefully, you can rule this guy in…or out. I'll let you get to it." He turned to leave as they opened the door to the Interview Room. The pair took seats across from the glum looking Landry. "Okay," began Robyn. "Tell us all about your relationship with Judith Winstone. Remember, Mr. Landry, in this instance, the truth may literally set you free."

For the next hour and fifteen minutes, Landry - in precise detail - told the entire story of his involvement with Judith Winstone. The two detectives hardly spoke, except to have him clarify a point here and there. At the end of the narrative, he was openly weeping over the loss of his friend, Judith, and the probable loss of his other friend, Ben Winstone.

Sean and Robyn stepped out to discuss what he had told them. Then they went to the Chief's office. Robyn was first to speak. "He's innocent, Chief. I'm sure of it. If anything, he's just another victim in this mess."

"I totally agree with Robyn," added Sean. "He was seduced by a beautiful, irresistible woman. I don't know if I could have avoided the same outcome. And look at what I've got at home." The Chief smiled wryly in acknowledgement.

"Anyway," continued a blushing Robyn, "I recommend we drop him as a suspect. Further, we don't reveal any of this to the Senator. What good could possibly come of it?"

"Agreed," said the obviously relieved Chief. "Go tell Mr. Landry the good news."

** ** **

Sean dropped Robyn off at Kris' house. He was headed to Home Depot to check out the big sale on snow blowers. His tired, ten-year-old model definitely needed to be replaced. Not something Robyn needed - or wanted - to be a part of.

She knocked on the side door then heard Kris, "C'mon in, the door's unlocked…I'm in the kitchen." Robyn pulled out a stool at the Breakfast Bar, as Kris was tending the Keurig. "I'm having coffee, want a cup?"

"Sure…where's Tom?"

"Oh, he's at the hospital helping a colleague with a hip replacement procedure. He'll be home in a couple of hours."

"On a *Saturday? After a funeral?*"

"I know. Weird, right? Don't know the details, but it was a last-minute thing." Kris fixed her coffee then started a cup for her friend. "So, what's new with you I don't already know?"

Robyn informed Kris about yesterday's meeting with Molly concerning Brick. And the drug. What he had done to the women who worked for him. At first, Kris was aghast at his actions; then concluded it all fit very well with her emerging assessment of his character (or lack thereof).

"This guy is a real piece of work. There's a lot more going on in his head than just general stress. I can't shake the feeling that he's got something to do with his mother's death."

"How so?" Asked Kris.

"I don't have any solid reason. It's just a hunch. Call it intuition. Anyway, I'm gonna take a deeper dive into this character."

"Good for you," encouraged her friend. "Your intuition has been right way more than not."

Kris fixed Robyn's coffee and brought both cups over to the bar, handing Robyn her cup.

"Thanks, Kris. The other *new thing* is about Brick's drug."

Robyn related what Molly and Sue had told her about *Pandora.* And the positive experiences of Allison and Dana (in spite of Brick's subterfuge). Their almost unquenchable desire; the intensity of the physical sensations culminating in their "indescribable" orgasms. Kris sat in rapt attention, hanging on every word as Robyn retold their stories.

"Oh my god," said Kris, "and no side -effects?"

"Not so far, and we're talking four women, one monitored especially close. Except, I guess, for the total loss of inhibition - if you want to call that a *side-effect.*"

"Jesus, Robyn. As a psychiatrist, I've got to say, *fascinating!* As a woman, I'd love to personally have that particular experience." She looked over at Robyn who was wearing a *Cheshire cat* grin. Kris, appearing somewhat perplexed, asked, "What?"

Robyn reached into her purse, pulling out four packets of a white, powdery substance. Kris' hand went to her mouth. "Jesus Christ, is that…"

"…Brick's aphrodisiac drug? It is," Robyn verified. "Are you thinking what I'm thinking?"

"Oh my god," said Kris. "I mean *YES!* When can we do it? What about the guys?"

"As to when…we'll have to talk about that. The guys CANNOT take this drug, it's only for women. But they'll be fine, don't worry."

Chapter Fourteen

Robyn and Sean sat together on the loveseat in the Den, a semi-final match of the Australian Open Tournament currently displayed on their new state-of-the-art High-Definition TV they had gifted themselves with at Christmas. Neither one was actually *watching* the match.

Robyn was excited; very much looking forward to tonight's experiment with this new drug. Sean was also excited; albeit tempered by anxiety over how this new aphrodisiac-like substance would actually affect the women.

Earlier that afternoon, Robyn and Kris had decided to tell their men what Robyn had learned about this new substance, *Pandora;* how it had affected the other women, Molly vouching for its safety, albeit cautioning it doesn't work for males. Both women expressed - in no uncertain terms - their determination to see how it would affect them.

Sean pointed out that neither woman had any sexual issues; unlike Molly, who, no fault of her own, lacked a normal sex drive. *Those were the people for whom the drug was intended.*

"True, " agreed Tom, "but by wholly unplanned circumstance, the other 'normal' women had all enjoyed the best sexual experience of their lives. What's wrong with that? As long as there aren't any harmful effects, I don't see a problem."

"Then you really believe this thing is safe?" Pressed Sean.

"I do," reiterated Tom. "Molly Skye is a pharmaceutical research specialist with many years experience. Her level of training and expertise equals that of a nurse-practitioner. So, if she feels safe - *as a trial subject herself* - then I'm confident of its safety."

Kris suggested each couple get together and just see what happens. The two men agreed; admitting they were at once both intrigued and excited. Robyn suggested they all have dinner at her and Sean's home; then - as Kris had alluded to earlier, *see what happens.*

Three hours later at the Wilder residence, Robyn glanced at her watch; "I've gotta go check on the roast. They should be arriving in about fifteen minutes." Sean nodded acknowledgement before turning his attention back to the tennis match.

While she checked the status of the roast, Robyn thought about their men's reaction to this unique situation. *You'd think that Tom - a doctor - would be the more conservative one...but NO, it's Sean. And he loves sex, Always willing to try new things. Go figure. I'll get him loosened up with that Burgundy he likes so much. Another bonus, this is really good timing. Get our minds off the investigations - at least for a while. Monday morning will be here soon enough.* Just then, the doorbell rang. *Hmmm, early. Good. This is gonna be an interesting night.*

** ** **

LeBron Smith laid the Forensics Report on his bed stand. For the third time tonight. For the life of him, he couldn't see anything there that might offer a lead to pursue. For sure, there wasn't any connection to the Winstone woman. The murder scene was just over a mile from the Willow Street

Bus Stop, a known hang-out for hookers. He decided tomorrow he'd take a more detailed look-see at the bus stop. He wondered what was taking so long getting the DNA results from all the semen stains. The problem there, of course, was that most likely multiple individuals were involved, given her profession. No matter, at least it was *something* - better than the *nothing* of the moment. He lay back in his bed, un-muting the sound of the Boston Bruins/New York Rangers hockey game happening in the background.

**. **. **

While LeBron Smith was at home mulling over the Patricia O'Brien murder, Jean LeFleur sat on his bunk in the Hillsboro County Jail. *How can I prove I'm innocent? I told those detectives the truth when they arrested me. I think the lady believed me. God, she's gorgeous; what the hell is she doing in the detective business? She should be in the movies. Makes me think about my Sadie. Saturday night and no Sadie. I wonder if she'll come visit me tomorrow. Gonna see the Judge Monday. He should get me a Public Defender. Damn sure not gonna get any bail.*

**. **. **

Molly was standing in front of the kitchen sink, wiping dry the last of the dinner dishes. She was thinking back to yesterday's discussion she and Sue had with Robyn, wondering if she had decided to try the drug for herself. Suddenly she felt something press against her ass.

She turned to look at Ted. "Do you have a boner?" she asked.

He grinned sheepishly.

Glancing at his crotch, she said, "You *DO* have a boner. What are you gonna do with that thing?" She suddenly realized she was very aroused. More to the point, *Without a Dose.*

Ted grabbed her by the shoulders, pulling her close. "Why, I'm gonna stick it in your ass, lady!"

**. **. **

Robyn poured Sean his third glass of Chardonnay, handing it to him. "I'm gonna have to cut you off after this one, Babe. You know, before it becomes a potential *performance* issue."

Looking across the table at Tom, Kris said, "I'll second that Honey. What - isn't that your third bottle of Heineken?" Both men conceded with a nod. "But what about you two?" Asked Tom.

Kris retorted, "We've had two glasses of Chardonnay apiece. And that's it for us, don't want to take any chances with our little *experiment.*"

"Speaking of which," said Sean, "It's been half an hour. Anything happening? Anybody?"

"Not yet," volunteered Kris. Robyn added, "They all said it kicks in at about an hour. Then after that, it's *Katie Bar the Door!*"

Tom had just begun a discussion about the now-completed location shooting of the movie, *One Last Chance* when he noticed Kris fidgeting with the top button of her blouse. Moreover, her stiffening nipples were pushing against the fabric. Tom stopped talking even as Sean took notice of both women's sudden change in demeanor. Robyn, now breathing heavily, glanced at him with an odd expression. Then Kris turned toward Robyn; putting her hands on Robyn's cheeks as she pulled her in for a kiss. Full on the mouth. Lips parting; tongues exploring.

The men looked at one another, astonished at the sight, getting excited. *Very excited.*

Tom loudly cleared his throat. "Ummm, Excuse me...*Ladies???*"

Kris pulled back from Robyn, at the same time removing her hand from her friend's left breast.

"Whoops!" Exclaimed Kris, "*Wrong person.*" She stood up and walked over to Tom, now also standing. She reached up to kiss him, simultaneously reaching down to his crotch to massage his stiffening cock.

"You know where the guest bedroom is," said Robyn coyly. She watched them head up the stairs and disappear down the hall. She turned toward Sean, "Coming...?" as she began ascending the stairs, bound for the Master Suite.

Kris was already naked and lying on the bed before Tom had shut the door. He was taken aback by her extreme arousal. Sure, she had always been a great sex partner, always an enthusiastic lover, but this...*this is beyond the pale.*

He pulled his jockey briefs down. No longer restrained, his stiff member bounced up and down for a second, amusing his waiting lover. "Come over here. I want you to do dirty, filthy, nasty things to me!" In a second, Tom was standing at the foot of the bed. She looked him up and down, before fixing her gaze on his cock, now standing at attention.

"Goddamn, Babe, *that's* what I call a Boner. Jesus, you could hammer nails with that thing!"

She took it between her thumb and forefinger, examining the appendage in much the way a doctor might. She moved her grip up the shaft slightly, then pulled back the foreskin, exposing the pink mushroom-like head. Suddenly, she let it go, taking it into her mouth. Kris began bobbing up and down over the full length of it before he pulled away, not wanting to cum yet. She laid back, spreading her legs wide. Tom pulled her back down to the foot of the bed then dropped to his knees, all the better to pleasure her pussy. He looked at her smooth mound, his excitement rising as he watched her labia slowly part; her erect clit emerging into view at the top of the cleft; the moist vaginal entrance just below opening tantalizing slow, inviting immediate penetration by…*anything.* She pulled his head toward her impatient pussy.

Needing no encouragement, Tom happily went to work, gently caressing her clit with his tongue while inserting a couple of fingers into her wet cunt. The increasing volume and intensity of her moaning alerted him to the approaching sexual cataclysm. Sure enough, she began bucking her hips as wave after wave of orgasmic pleasure washed over her. Still breathing heavily, she gently pushed him away. Slowly regaining composure as her spent body relaxed, she said, "That was the most intense orgasm - *orgasms*- I've ever had! The girls were *Not* exaggerating, not even a little." They lay still for a couple of minutes as her arousal once again approached a crescendo. She pulled him atop her, hoarsely whispering, "Your turn; *Fuck me! Fuck Me Hard! Fuck My Brains Out!!*" He plunged his rock-hard cock into her wet cunt, thrusting it in up to the hilt, then completely withdrawing before repeating. About fifteen strokes later, finally spent, she felt his cum jetting into her as she experienced a super-intense vaginal orgasm.

** ** **

Sean came out of the bathroom to find Robyn softly moaning as she alternately stuck two fingers in her pussy, then pulled out the newly moist digits to massage her clit. *In, Out, Rub, Repeat.* He became fixated on her masturbatory episode when she suddenly stopped.

"What's a girl to do when she's horny and no man's around to service her?" She asked playfully. Robyn gazed at his erect cock. She subtly touched herself as she continued to stare at it. She thought, *He has a beautiful cock. Nicely shaped head. I love the slight curve of the shaft - really sexy - plus it's pretty fucking thick. Eight inches fully hard. Almost. Seven and nine-tenths. That was a pretty cool session - the night we took a ruler to it. And he worked it all the way in. I remember how exciting it was watching him stroke me. Plus, that was the first time he fucked me in the ass. Took a lot to encourage him. Said he wasn't much for ass fucking, but he did seem to enjoy it that night. Just as well...He's a bit too long - and thick - for my ass. It's quite a stretch with him...*Robyn laughed out loud at her unintended pun.

While Robyn was doing a mental evaluation of her spouse's penis; he was looking her over, again appreciating how lucky he was to have such a beautiful wife. Perfect in every way: nice, firm tits topped with a pair of dark brown nipples, easily protruding a half inch when hard. Flat tummy above her mound, covered in a thick thatch of pubic hair; now comes the *piece d' resistance* - her pussy; meaty lips parting just enough to expose the swollen clit perched above her vagina - open a tiny bit, teasing the imagination. He noticed her hand once again disappearing into the thicket between her legs. He was startled when she suddenly started laughing. Alarmed, he asked, "What's wrong?"

"Oh, I was just thinking back to the time when we measured your cock, you kept insisting it was eight inches when the ruler showed one-tenth less. Then you said, *What - Am I auditioning for a porn movie?* We both cracked up, remember? Just before we fucked our brains out."

"Right," said Sean. Recalling the incident, he began laughing himself.

"Come over here *Big Boy*," beckoned his wife. A minute later he had her hands pinned to the mattress, his cock disappearing into the supple forest between her spread-wide legs.

..** **

Kris looked over at her partner…her erstwhile lover. Out like the proverbial light. That third Heineken did it. She knew once he got off, he'd be done for the rest of the night. Two Heinekens, Okay. She might be able to rouse him. *Three* Heinekens - out of the question. It would take a three alarm, 911-style emergency to get him up and moving. Her arousal level, still at about a twelve on a ten-scale, set her mind off in a new direction. *It would be great to have a session with Sean. AND ROBYN.* For the first time in her life, she allowed her bi-sexual urge free reign. All her life, she had found herself sexually attracted to a particular woman here or there. She had *always* suppressed those feelings immediately. Not this time.

Molly had told Robyn, *the only "side-effect" of the drug was Loss of Inhibition.*

She was right. *If I ever wanted to have sex with a woman, it would be Robyn Wilder. My best friend. My former boyfriend's wife. This is my one shot. That lady is so fucking hot…I've got to have her, even if it means fucking Sean again (Poor Me) to create a "three-way" scenario for justification.* Kris headed down the hall; upon reaching their bedroom, she listened for a moment. Silence. She knocked tentatively, then heard Robyn say, "C'mon in."

Kris opened the door. They were both naked, laying side-by-side on pillows propped up against the headboard. Robyn had the body she had imagined. Perfect. Sean looked just as good as back in the day, his long cock, flaccid at the moment, resting on his left thigh.

"Where's Tom," inquired Sean, anticipating a possible four-way fuck-fest.

"Dead to the world," said Kris, "And he will be until tomorrow morning. *I'm* still horny though. *Real horny.* I was thinking maybe you guys might be up for a little three-way action."

Robyn suddenly perked right up. "I think that's a great idea. I've never made it with a woman before, especially with one as beautiful as you Kris." Robyn got up, heading to the bathroom and the bidet'.

"Well. Sean," asked Kris, "are you in? Gotta say, I wouldn't mind getting that big thing of yours inside me one more time."

"What about Tom? Do you think he'd be Okay with this?"

"I do," confirmed Kris. "But he doesn't *necessarily* have to know. On the other hand, I have no problem discussing it with him later."

"Good enough for me," he replied. "But you girls go ahead; have your fun. I just want to rest - and watch - for a while. Maybe catch up along the way," he teased, just as Robyn emerged from the bathroom. Sean got up and crossed the room, taking a seat in a rocker opposite the bed. Both women climbed on the bed at the same time.

Robyn gazed at her friend's face, really appreciating how truly beautiful she was. She let her eyes wander down; nice supple breasts, smaller than her own, still just perfect. Robyn could see the smooth mound above her pussy, concealed for the moment between her closed legs.

Kris glanced at Robyn's ample, but firm tits. She was treated to the sight of her dark brown nipples growing hard right before her eyes. *Jesus,* thought Kris, *those are some big nips. Got to nibble on those.* Looking further down, she spied the triangle of dark brown hair just above her pubic area. *That's a surprise. Always imagined her with a clean-shaven pussy. This is gonna be interesting.*

Robyn touched Kris' cheek; then both leaned in for a long, wet kiss. Kris pulled her in tight, feeling Robyn's stiff nipples pressing into her breasts, her own nipples immediately growing hard in response. Both women lay back, spreading their legs as they assumed the familiar "69" position. Robyn parted the smooth lips of Kris' pussy, amazed at how wet her cunt was. Robyn latched onto the smallish, but hard, nub that was Kris' clit. The subsequent loud moaning signaled the oncoming series of orgasms. After Kris came, she rolled Robyn onto her back, using her hands to spread her thighs wide apart; in the process, affording Sean an excellent look at the proceedings.

Kris was immediately surprised with her view of Robyn's genitals. She had anticipated some difficulty, given her friend's thick bush. To the contrary, her pink, meaty labia were already parted, exposing the opening of her wet cunt, inviting immediate penetration. Then Robyn's erect clit poking out from the thicket caught her eye. Kris buried her face in Robyn's pussy, quickly moving to her swollen clit, licking and sucking for all she was worth.

Sean, who had been intently watching the goings-on, was slowly stroking his rock-hard cock, being careful not to allow the onset of an unwanted ejaculation. He watched with increasing excitement as his wife became caught up in a series of orgasmic contractions.

He got up and went over to the bed, telling Kris to get up on her knees. She quickly assumed the position as he rammed his cock, doggy-style, into her cunt. She moaned - he grunted. Then Robyn reached over, using her hand to pull his cock out of Kris. She sucked on it for a moment before re-inserting it into Kris' pussy. Again, Robyn pulled it out, but before she could get it back in her mouth, she felt it pulsate; his cum spraying everywhere as she continued to stroke it. Finally emptied, she let it go; the three of them falling back on the bed, satiated.

Chapter Fifteen

Sean sat at the kitchen table scanning the front page of the *Sunday News,* while Kris, seated across from him, contentedly sipped her coffee. Robyn was busy with breakfast preparations, moving the final stack of blueberry pancakes over to the serving platter. She checked the bacon, pronouncing it now at the perfect crispiness; its delicious smell wafting through the entire kitchen, prompting Sean to ask, "Where the hell is Tom? I'm so hungry, my stomach thinks my throat's been cut." He looked up, relieved to see Tom finally coming down the stairs.

"Perfect timing," observed Robyn.

"*Something* smells good!" Exclaimed Tom as he approached the table, taking the seat next to Kris. Robyn set the still-steaming platter of pancakes at the center of the table, then headed back for the bacon. In what seemed an instant, the two stacks of eight had made their way to four separate plates. The room was quiet for the next ten minutes as the group made short work of their breakfast.

"Jesus," observed Kris, "I didn't realize how hungry I was," the other three quickly agreeing with her assessment. "Considering last night's activity - I'm not surprised. Talk about calorie-burn…," the observation sparking a round of laughter.

"For a fact," interrupted Tom, "I don't know about you guys - glancing at Sean and Robyn - but we crashed around midnight; end-of-story until nine this morning." The other three exchanged quick glances, silently acknowledging their earlier decision to keep their little *3-way orgy* to themselves - at least for the time being.

Robyn stood up. "More coffee anyone?"

..**

Brick's eyelids fluttered for a moment as he slowly awoke. He propped himself up on his elbows, looking around. *I'm in my old bedroom at the mansion. Wait. What time is it? WHAT DAY IS IT?*

He scoured his mind, desperately trying to call up a recent memory - *any memory* - of what had been happening to him. *Mother is dead, I know that. But how did that happen?* He vaguely recalled talking with his father - about what, he hadn't a clue. *What the hell is going on??* Panic, like the bile in his throat, was slowly rising; sure to spiral out of control very soon. "Hello? Is anyone out there? Hello! HELLO!!! HELLO!!!" Just then, the door opened.

..**

The Correctional Officer pushed open the cell door. "You've got a visitor, Le Fleur. Follow me."

He led the inmate to the Search Room where he was ordered to remove all his clothes. Once naked, he was instructed to raise his arms over his head. An Officer had him open his mouth, using a small flashlight to inspect its interior. Then he was ordered to turn around, bend over, and spread his legs. Next, he heard the tell-tale snap of a plastic glove. *Oh, good,* he sarcastically thought, *here comes my favorite part.* The officer said, "Put your clothes back on."

He was led over to a table in the corner where he was told to "sit." A moment later the entrance door to the Visitors Room opened. An Officer escorted Sadie over to his table. She took the chair opposite him, offering him a big smile as she sat down. Le Fleur was grateful she had come. He had no family. *Sure, she's just a hooker, but she's got a heart of gold.*

LeFleur smiled right back. "Thanks for coming, Sadie. I really, really appreciate it. So…*Adams.* Your last name. Didn't even know that until I saw your visitor application." He reached over to enfold her hands with his, when suddenly…

"HEY! No contact allowed!"

LeFleur turned around, "Sorry Officer, it won't happen again." He turned back toward Sadie silently mouthing, *Asshole.* She winked at him. "So, it's not looking too good for Yours Truly. But I feel like the lady detective believes I didn't kill the woman, let alone rape her."

"Well, at least that's good," said Sadie. "They don't think you had anything to do with Pat's murder, right?"

Looking confused, he asked, "*Who* is Pat?"

"Patricia O'Brien. The girl what got raped and killed last week."

"You know…*knew* her?" Asked a suddenly intrigued LeFleur.

"Yeah, for about a year now. Nice girl - real smart - but she got all fucked up with drugs and was workin' the streets to pay for that. She'd been in college, was gonna be a doctor before she got involved with some guy - said he was a research scientist - who got her hooked-on speedballs. But that's not all. A couple of months ago he gave her a pill he said he was working on that would make women horny, so that they would really enjoy sex. She told me he wasn't lying. Said she was really getting off with her "Johns." She told me it was so good for her she would have done them for free. 'Course, she never did; needed the money too much."

"Sadie," asked a now excited LeFleur, "Would you be willing to tell that to the detectives working my case? It might really help out a lot with my own case!"

"Course I would, Jean. It would make me really happy if I could help you out." They spent the next hour getting to know more about one another. Finally, Sadie said she had to go. She was supposed to pick her sister up at the Greyhound Terminal in about fifteen minutes. He watched as she wrote down Robyn's name and cellphone number. Before she left, he once again expressed his heartfelt gratitude for her taking such an interest in him. Sadie smiled as she turned to leave, feeling a sudden warm sensation wash over her. She liked that feeling.

** ** **

After his father and the doctor (who by chance had just stopped by to check in with the Senator) left him alone, he took a shower then slipped into sweatpants and a sweater. He sat in the chair next to his bed, thinking about their visit. He told them he was fully aware of the time, place, people and who he was. He was unable to recall anything that had happened after the night of Matthew McNeil's birthday party at the Mansion. Doctor Reston told him he had a form of amnesia associated with experiencing a traumatic event, assuring him that eventually he would recover his full memory. Try as he might, he couldn't remember anything that happened over the previous ten days.

He suddenly realized he had an erection. *Where did THAT come from,* he wondered. He grabbed his phone and called Allison McKenna to invite her over for (*what - sex?)* lunch (*then* sex*)*. She politely declined, saying she had previous plans. He laid his phone back on the table. *Now what?* He thought. *Well, I can't sit here with a hard-on the rest of the day.* He stood up, let his sweatpants drop to his ankles, grabbed his cock, and gave it a good wanking. Done, he went into the bathroom, fetching a towel to clean up his mess.

..**

The four of them were engaged in an enthusiastic review of the previous evening's "activities" when Kris held up her hand. "Stop!" She commanded. "This isn't working out quite the way I had envisioned. You know, have a rational discussion about how we all felt at the time, especially when compared to our normal encounters - but I just can't seem to be able to achieve objectivity - still too much residual horniness. And talking about it just gets me more aroused."

Robyn nodded in agreement before suggesting they come up with some sort of plan for the upcoming week. That might help all of them shift focus from sex to the murder investigations.

Except for Tom, he wasn't involved with any of that. He did, however, have Emergency Room duty later today, specifically, 3:00 P.M. to midnight. Robyn's phone buzzed. She looked at the unfamiliar number on the screen before accepting the call. With a quizzical expression, she said, "Yes?"

On the other end the caller said, "Hello, Mrs. Wilder. This is Sadie Adams. You don't know me - I'm a friend of Jean LeFleur's. He asked me to call you. I have information that may be helpful in the investigation of the Patricia O'Brien murder."

Robyn held up a hand, telling the group, "I've got to take this." Turning, she disappeared down the hall, returning about four minutes later. Robyn related what Sadie had just told her; Kris and Sean quickly becoming excited, especially Sean.

"This could be the break we've been looking for!" Enthused Sean. We've got to get ahold of LeBron and read him in on this right away!"

Before Sean could continue, Kris' phone rang. Caller I.D. displayed *Sue Alvarez*. She announced, "It's Sue Alvarez," then answered the phone, "Hello, Sue…"

..**

Kris pulled into Sue's driveway and shifted into Park. During the trip over, she thought over what Sue had told her about an earlier phone call with Allison McKenna. Apparently, Brick had asked her over for lunch, but Allison suspected the underlying motive was sex. She knew Brick had had some sort of mental breakdown at yesterday's funeral service, adding to her anxiety. Kris had originally planned on interviewing Brick tomorrow, then the four women, but after Sue's call she suggested the two of them talk today; Sue agreeing it was a good idea.

Sue stood at the door, waving Kris to come in. She took Kris' coat before leading her into the living room where she sat on the sofa opposite Sue. Kris looked the woman over: petite, probably about 5'1' or so, much shorter than herself. *Nice body,* she thought, *very sexy looking. Wait - what the hell is going on...I'm still being influenced by the drug. Well, fortunately, THAT was the original topic of this interview; might as well get right to it.*

"Thanks for seeing me today. Before we start, I need to let you know I will be recording our conversation for my official report. But this report is highly confidential...any information provided to a third party will be anonymous. Is that okay with you?"

"Sure...yes, of course," confirmed Sue. "If it helps take down this asshole."

"First," continued Kris, "I'd like to discuss this *Pandora* drug he created and its aphrodisiac-like effects. And, for the record, is it a fact that you were covertly dosed without prior consent?"

Sue provided chapter and verse about what they did, how she felt at the time, including her complete loss of inhibition.

"So, how long did these intense sexual urges last? One day? Two days? Longer?" While Sue was giving it some serious thought, she found herself becoming aroused by this beautiful creature across from her. A tall, blue-eyed blonde with a great body. Probably ten years older than herself, but in great shape. She felt her nipples, unrestrained by a bra, growing hard.

"You know...probably three days total. The second day, about 50% less, then the third day another 25% drop."

Kris reached for her phone and paused the recording function. She looked directly at Sue, noticing her nipples straining against the fabric of her blouse. "I've got to be honest with you Sue. Last night Robyn and I took a dose, mostly out of curiosity. We rationalized that we were doing it for *research* purposes. Anyway, we had what you might call an orgy of sorts."

"For the first time ever, I indulged my desire to make it with a woman. Who happened to be my best friend. It was incredible. Normally, I would never tell you, or anyone, what I had done. Or the fact that I'm still horny as hell and have an incredible urge to bury my head between your legs. I feel like I'm in some kind of fantasy porn movie. *Talk about having no inhibitions.*"

Sue stood up, telling Kris to "Follow me." She led her into the bedroom. In less than a minute, both women were totally naked. They continued standing, each drinking in the other's body.

Sue lay back on the bed, longing to be touched all over - *ravished* - by this mature beauty standing over her. Kris let her eyes wander over the petite woman below her. *Nice nipples, tight body, perfect legs...what's it like in between them?* she wondered; her excitement mounting.

Kris settled over her, grasping Sue's hands, then spreading her arms wide. She bent down to kiss her, Sue opening her mouth, inviting her lover's tongue to mingle with her own. Kris moved down a bit, planting gentle little kisses on either side of her neck before moving one hand to her right breast, cupping it as she used her palm to caress the long nipple, eliciting a soft moan from her lover. She turned her attention to the other breast, taking it into her mouth, using her tongue to fold it in half; Sue now moaning more loudly as Kris suddenly released the nipple, watching it spring back to its full erect length.

Kris continued her downward trek, slowly sliding off the foot of the bed onto her knees, simultaneously using her hands to spread Sue's thighs wide apart. Suddenly she held still, astounded by what she saw. Sue had a nice, smooth pubis with thick pussy lips - not as meaty as Robyn's, she noticed - but her clitoris, it was...*huge.* It looked like a miniature cock, proportionately perfect. The longer Kris looked at it, the more aroused she became. She knew her own clit was as hard as it ever had been but paled in comparison to Sue's unique nub.

Sue looked at Kris. "*I know,* I always get that the first time I'm with a woman - *or man.* Just a *freak-of nature* thing, but everybody seems to like it. I know I do. Want to touch it? Here, watch." Sue grasped her clit between her thumb and forefinger, slowly retracting the foreskin, exposing a perfectly shaped mushroom-like head, just like a man's - only smaller. Sue took Kris' hand, encouraging her to touch it. Kris gripped it in the same manner Sue had. Then, she began stroking it in the same fashion she would have masturbated Tom. Sue began groaning loudly...*I'm gonna cum, I'M GONNA CUM!* Kris reached down with her free hand, finding her own clit; she began rubbing furiously, bringing herself to a super-intense orgasm.

She climbed back onto the bed, laying quietly next to her lover. After about five minutes, Sue said, "Now let me do my thing. Payback is gonna be a *pleasure,* I promise." She began touching Kris all over, at the same time planting little kisses. She paid special attention to her breasts, alternately sucking, then lightly, biting the stiff nipples. Finally, she spread Kris' legs wide, skillfully using her fingers to massage her labia, before pushing two, three, then four fingers into her wet, ever-widening pussy. Kris yelled," More!" Obligingly, Sue plunged her whole fist into Kris' stretched-to-the-max cunt, Kris moaning and grunting loudly in her unprecedented orgasmic pleasure.

The women cleaned up then relaxed for a bit, enjoying some wine before Kris re-activated the tape for the official record, documenting an hour's worth of Brick's abusive, coercive…and yes, criminal behavior.

..****

LeBron tossed his coat on the chair by the door, then headed into the kitchen to snag a cold brew before watching the four o'clock edition of *Sports Center*. A profile of his namesake, LeBron James, was scheduled.

As he waited for the commercial break to finish, he reflected on his just completed trip to the Willow Street Bus Stop. His "second look" turned up empty, which wasn't surprising. But, it was worth a shot, like the Lottery Ticket saying, "If you don't play, you can't win." He popped open the can and was about to settle back in his chair when his cellphone vibrated. It was Sean Wilder calling. He hit the mute button.

"Hello, Sean…no, no bother at all…WHAT! HOLY SHIT, THAT IS GOOD NEWS!…No, I don't know her, at least by name…sure, 10 o'clock in your office sounds great…I will now, and you have a great day as well. See ya tomorrow at ten. Bye." He ended the call and put his phone on the adjacent end table.

Smith was absolutely delighted. *First break in the case* ran through his mind. *Sean sounded real optimistic; I'm really looking forward to the interview.* Smiling, he picked up the remote and un-muted the TV. Then, he took a long pull on his *Coors Lite* before settling back to enjoy the program.

Chapter Sixteen

At 9:00 A.M. sharp, Senator Winstone walked into the parlor with Brick. He glanced over at Kris, who stood up as he walked into the room.

"Brick, this is Doctor Kris Wood, a psychiatrist who has been retained by the District Attorney's Office to interview everyone close to your mother, which of course includes the Winstone family. This is a routine part of homicide investigations."

Brick eyed the Doctor with some suspicion; quickly overshadowed by a rising sexual interest in the woman. *God, SHE'S HOT! Great body, nice tits…I'd love to fuck her.* Then he realized his cock was beginning to get hard. *Damn it. It's times like this when I wished I had a normal size dick. Pretty tough hiding this thing when it's stiff.*

Kris walked over with her right hand extended. She immediately took notice of his erection but made a point of averting her eyes. "Good morning, Mr. Winstone, it's a pleasure to meet you. As your father said, this is a purely routine interview, you shouldn't infer otherwise."

Brick bowed slightly. Using what charm he could muster, he said, "The pleasure is all mine, Doctor Wood. I'm happy to answer any questions you may have."

Kris returned to her seat as the Senator headed toward the door. "Well," he said with a smile, "I'll leave you to it Doctor."

After the Senator closed the door, Brick took a seat opposite Kris, trying to sneak in an *up-skirt* peak between her legs before she crossed them.

Kris immediately detected his sexual interest in her, deciding to use it to her advantage. "So, Mr. Winstone…"

Brick cut in, "Please - call me *Brick,* I'd feel more comfortable with less formality."

"Of course, *Brick,* " she confirmed, "My primary objective is to ascertain the mental and emotional state of those closest to your mother. I understand you had a traumatic reaction during the funeral service, serious enough to require medical intervention."

"Uh, yes, that's true Doctor Wood. Let me ask you…*just how confidential* is what I tell you during this interview?"

"Unless it pertains to the circumstances of your mother's death, whatever you reveal to me about your physical and *mental* health is fully protected by the medical confidentiality laws."

"Well, that's good to know," said an obviously relieved Brick. "You're a shrink…er, psychiatrist, right?"

"I am indeed. I have a private practice specializing in relationship therapy and treating sexual dysfunction. I don't deal with the physical side of dysfunction issues."

"Ah," replied Brick, slowly nodding. "And you say anything I tell you here is confidential?"

"Unless you're discussing a crime, *Yes.* You are protected by doctor/patient confidentiality." Kris was gaining his trust. She was already aware of his sexual attraction toward her. Very subtly, she uncrossed her legs, allowing her skirt to ride up her thighs ever so slightly as she very slowly parted her legs, affording him a "teasing" kind of view that should stimulate his imagination.

Brick considered her answer to his confidentiality question; at the same time noticing that at some point she had uncrossed her legs. He nonchalantly glanced at her slightly spread legs…he could *almost* see her panties, his cock once again growing hard in response.

** ** **

Molly, somewhat nervous about what the CEO wanted, stepped into his office. McNeil immediately stood; smiling, he said, "Good morning, Molly! Come in, come in. Please have a seat," motioning toward the chair facing his desk. She took a seat, feeling more comfortable; sensing his friendly demeanor was genuine.

"Molly, I'll get straight to the point. The reason I called you in was to ask you to temporarily head up the research department. Obviously, Brick is unable to work in any capacity for the moment…actually, for the foreseeable future. I am suspending the *Pandora* trial until further notice. I do, however, want a complete written summation of what has happened to this point."

Molly appeared about to say something when McNeil held up his hand. "I believe I know what you want to bring up about Brick. You should know, *I am Aware*. I would ask you to put *those* issues on the back burner for the moment. Be assured; you will very much be a part of that eventual conversation. You're smart, well-liked, and most definitely have leadership qualities. I need you to help 'steady the ship,' so to speak, through this short-term turbulence."

Molly swelled with pride to think that Mr. McNeil had such confidence in her. "You can count on me, Mr. McNeil. I'll do my best."

"I'm sure you will, Molly. I am sending out a memo to all staff informing them of your new position. Thank you for your loyalty to Delta Pharma." They both stood; then McNeil suddenly said, "Oh, I almost forgot. Kris Wood, a local Psychiatrist, has been retained by the D.A.'s Office as a consultant in the investigation. I know her, she's good people - also a good friend of Robyn Wilder. Anyway, she's requested to speak briefly with you, Allison McKenna, and Dana Bryce. I'd like you to get in touch with them. I've reserved the Conference Room for that purpose from noon until 2:00 P.M. Also, there will be a catered lunch served at 12:30."

Molly smiled, saying, "I'll take care of it Mr. McNeil...and thank you for the lunch." She turned to leave, still feeling all warm and fuzzy inside. *He really likes me,* she thought.

****.**.****

Robyn was first to enter the Interview Room, followed by Sean, then Detective Smith.

"Good morning, Miss Adams. I'm Robyn Wilder...we spoke on the phone yesterday. This is my husband Sean who is with the D.A.'s office, and this gentleman - she gestured toward Smith - is Detective LeBron Smith of the Manchester P.D. First, Thank you for coming in."

"You can call me Sadie. I ain't no lady, just plain folks. I don't know if what I say is gonna help you people or not, but I'm here 'cause of Jean. He's my friend. He said I could trust you-all, especially the lady detective. Said if I help you, you might could help him out."

"I'll be honest with you Sadie," said Robyn. "Mr. LeFleur committed a crime - a serious crime. That said, if he's honest with us, I guarantee all of us will do the best we can for him, regardless of if your information helps us or not."

"Good enough for me, Missus; fire away!"

"First I must tell you that this interview is being recorded," said Smith as he reached over and turned on the recorder. "This is Detective LeBron Smith, an officer of the Manchester Police Department and Lead Investigator of the Patricia O'Brien homicide. Participating in this interview are Investigator Sean Wilder of the Hillsboro County District Attorney's Office, and Private Investigator Robyn Wilder who has been deputized by the Manchester P.D. Miss Sadie Adams has come forward to offer information - of her own free will - in the aforementioned case."

Sean began the interview. "Sadie, why don't you tell us what knowledge you have concerning the murder of Patricia O'Brien. We might interrupt you here and there to clarify a point."

"Sure, yeah," she began, "I met Pat - Patricia - about a year ago…" Sadie went on to relate how they became friends; how she was sad that Pat was in the prostitute business to support "her goddam drug habit," how she tried and failed numerous times to get the young woman off the drugs, she figured getting away from the streets would follow. Sadie related how "whip-smart" the girl was; couldn't stand seeing such a smart, pretty girl waste her life like this.

At this point, Robyn interrupted her. "You told me on the phone yesterday that she told you her street situation started with some guy she met in college. Could you give us more details about that?"

"Sure," replied Sadie. "It was this guy that fucked up her life so much." Sadie related in great detail what Pat had told her. "This guy at college - said he was a research scientist - at first got her hooked-on cocaine, then those heroin speedball things. He supplied a lot of her drugs, when she ran out of money, she paid him off in bed. Eventually, it got so bad, she got kicked out of college, ending up on the streets."

"She didn't see him for a long while until one day he saw her at the Willow Street bus stop. Told her he come up with this new sex drug that made fucking always great, even with Johns. He gave her a pill. She stayed with him a couple of days, and the next time I saw her, she said he wasn't lying, it was the best sex she ever had. Said she came so many times, she lost count. Offered me a couple of pills, but I refused. One thing I never did was goddamn drugs."

Smith, barely able to control his excitement, asked her, "Do you know this guy's name? What he looks like? Did she ever say where he lived?"

"No, no…and no," answered Sadie. He never came round when I was with her. Never said what he looked like, either. Wait…she did say he had a huge cock, the biggest she had ever seen. Which a 'course, she liked - like any woman would," this last said with a wry smile.

"Wait - and she made a comment about how his big cock made up a little for his lack of looks."

"Did she talk much about how the drug affected her?" Asked Robyn.

"Matter a fact, she did," replied Sadie, rubbing her chin. "Said it was the best drug she ever took specially when ya think about gettin' a bang for your buck." Sadie suddenly laughed aloud at her unintended pun, then continued; "I mean, she got really detailed about it, like talking 'bout how wet she got, how sensitive her little girl-thing, what do they call it…"

"A clitoris, *clit* for short," offered Robyn.

"…Yeah, yeah - that's it - her *clit* - how it got all swelled up just thinking about sex. Said they fucked for hours at a time. Then, she shocked the shit outta me. Asked if I ever had sex with a woman. She got real disappointed when I said I didn't want to do that. Just old-fashioned man woman sex for me. Don't get me wrong, I like sucking cock and gettin' my pussy licked, but lesbian sex, nuh-uh. Not my bag."

"So that changed her even more?" Asked Robyn.

"Yes, it did," confirmed Sadie. "Her Johns loved it. She'd fuck-em another time or two *for free.*"

Sadie allowed that she couldn't recall anything more and hoped that they would catch the sick son-of-a-bitch that killed her friend. As Sadie prepared to leave, all three detectives thanked her profusely, telling her the information she provided was *very helpful.*

** ** **

Brick continued looking across at Kris, his arousal slowly increasing. He broke what was becoming - at least for him - an uncomfortable silence. "So, I can say things in complete confidentiality, right?"

"Again, yes. As long as it has nothing to do with a crime."

"Okay, then. It's about me and how I feel about sex. That won't make you uncomfortable?"

"No, Brick, *I'm a psychiatrist.* I specialize in resolving sexual dysfunction." In spite of herself, Kris was also becoming aroused (*The drug is STILL affecting me*). For the first time in her career, she was having difficulty maintaining objectivity.

"Well," he began, "I'm like *Oversexed.* It's almost always - at the very least - in the back of my mind. Like you, for instance - *and I'm NOT coming on to you* - I get an erection just looking at you. Thinking, you know - what would you look like naked; how would it feel to touch you all over; how you would feel on the inside…"

Kris worked hard to maintain a neutral expression even as she felt the wetness in her panties while her nipples grew stiff (Thank God she was wearing a bra). *This is definitely the goddamn drug. I damn sure don't find this guy attractive, not even a little. But his cock…judging from the bulge in his crotch that thing is HUGE.*

"Okay," interrupted Kris, "I understand what you mean about being *oversexed,* but for the moment, we have to keep it within the parameters of the investigation. For instance, did you ever have sexual feelings toward your mother?"

"GOD, NO!" He exclaimed loudly. "I'm not *that* sick," he lied. Immediately his erection went away, caught off guard by Kris' sobering inquiry. For Kris' part, ironically, she had only asked the question to re-focus his attention away from her. Which apparently had worked.

Kris ended the interview prematurely, feigning a sudden migraine headache. She apologized, assuring him they would resume at a later time. After she left, she asked the Butler for the nearest bathroom. Once inside, she had a good pee. As she wiped herself, she couldn't help but notice her pussy was extra wet. She inserted a couple of fingers, then moved the moist digits up and out, caressing her labia before furiously rubbing her clit, quickly climaxing.

Brick returned to his room. Locking the door, he dropped his pants, grabbing his once again solid cock. Before he reached ten strokes, he was spilling his seed everywhere.

**. **. **

Finished with the final call, Molly laid her phone back on the desk, relieved that both women were available for the lunchtime interview session on such short notice. She was curious about why Sue Alvarez hadn't been included. She was, after all, a part of the *exploited* women.

**. **. **

After Sadie left the room, the Investigators sat quietly for a few moments, LeBron finally breaking the silence. "IT'S BRICK! IT'S GODDAMN BRICK!" He said excitedly as he stood up.

"Wait…hold on partner," said Sean. "I'm not disagreeing with you, but we've got to tread carefully here. We're talking *circumstantial,* in the broadest sense of the word."

"I agree with Sean," offered Robyn. "You're right, LeBron. He's the one. But we've gotta be smart about nailing this bastard. What we've got legally so far is…squat. Plus, he's *got an alibi.* Let's not let our exuberance get in the way of good detective work."

"You guys are right of course, just got caught up in the moment," admitted the detective. "Let's nail this prick. I suggest we put a tail on him just in case he leaves the Mansion."

"Right," agreed Sean. "Assign somebody that's good. Someone who won't *get made.* Now I've got to go see Dave Wozniak. We should keep this quiet for the moment, not tip our hand."

"I've got to touch base with Chief Daughtery. And I agree with the keeping quiet part."

"So, what's on your agenda, Robyn?" Asked her husband.

"I think I'll give Kris a call and see how her interview with Brick turned out."

****. **. ****

Sue sat on her sofa, looking out at the stand of Birch trees at the edge of her property. It was a nice, sunny day, unusually warm for this time of year. The weather guy said it would reach 55 degrees. Must be the "January thaw." Makes up for that bitter cold a week ago. I remember how much Dana was bitching about it. Then again, she *is* a Florida girl.

Her thoughts turned to *Pandora*. She still had twelve doses of the original eighteen she had "appropriated." Five powder form and seven pills. She was beginning to question the merits of the drug. Sure, the physical part was terrific. But the *inhibition* thing. That bothered her. Like that was a sort of boundary guard on peoples' behavior.

Chapter Seventeen

Brick sat in his chair watching the maid make the bed. His cock was getting hard. Again.

Maria Sanchez was a forty-something woman who had been working for the family some eight years now. Brick gave her a quick once-over. Average looking (had nice full lips, perfect for sucking cock) dark hair, brown eyes, *really* big tits; overall a pretty good body, though a tad on the thick side (*beggars can't be choosers,* drifted through his mind). He made his decision.

"Hey Maria, would you fix me a coffee? Make one for yourself, too. I'd like to have a little chat, if it's okay with you. I'm really feeling pretty lonely."

"Si', er, *Yes,* Mr. Winstone." She mostly spoke Spanish, but her English was quite good. Maria felt sorry for Brick…all that had happened to him lately. She brought their coffees over, setting them on the table next to his chair.

"Would you kindly bring me the box of Kleenex by the coffeemaker?" As she left to fetch the tissues, he quickly emptied a packet of *Pandora* into her coffee; watching it dissolve almost instantly. When she returned, he indicated she take the chair on the other side of the table. While they drank their coffees, he brought up her family, feigning interest in her husband; expressing dismay at her infertility - so sad, she badly wanted children. He listened as she went on about her ten-year younger sister who lived with them.

Brick looked at his watch, "Goodness, Maria, it's almost noon. Why don't you go have lunch. The doctor is coming in to check on me in a few minutes. You should come back in about an hour to finish what little there is to do - maybe we can talk some more."

"Thank you, Mr. Winstone, I would like that very much. See you then." *Such a nice man,* she thought. *And really nice-looking, too.* For just a second, she wondered why *that* had crossed her mind.

****.**.****

Molly, Allison, and Dana were already seated at the conference table when Kris came into the room. "Sorry I'm late, I went to the wrong building first time around. Anyway, I'm happy to finally meet you all. You must be Molly," as she extended her hand. "You made quite an impression on my friend, Robyn."

Molly, in turn, introduced the women. "Doctor Wood, this is Allison McKenna, the firm's accountant and *this* is Dana Bryce, Brick's secretary." Kris smiled as she shook hands with each of the women in turn.

"Please, if it's Okay, I'd really rather use first names. Just *Kris* is fine for me," everyone quickly agreeing. The three women sat as Kris continued, "I've got to record some portions of our meeting - part of my consultation agreement with the D.A.'s Office – but," she glanced coyly around the room as she finished setting up her MacBook - "there's another issue we're going to have to address." Smiling; Molly, Allison, and Dana exchanged knowing glances.

****.**.****

Brick had been waiting patiently when he heard a knock on the door. *Ah,* he thought, *here's my girl - and it's just her and me* (the Butler had the afternoon off). "Come in," he cheerfully invited. Maria stepped in, walking over to where he was sitting on the edge of the bed. She stood silent; her hands folded in front of her apron.

Brick noticed her flushed appearance, the heavy breathing. She looked at him with an odd expression, her eyes drifting to the growing bulge in his pants. She didn't try to conceal where her attention was focused. "Are you feeling all right, Maria?"

She looked right at him. "I find you so handsome, Mr. Winstone. I apologize for my behavior; I just can't seem to help myself."

He looked at her. "I understand Maria. We all have needs. Let me help you." He took her hand, guiding it to his fully erect cock. She began running her hand over his crotch, fumbling for the zipper. She unbuttoned his pants, then unzipped the fly before quickly pulling his pants down.

Her hand went to her mouth, gasping at her first sight of his massive member. She reached for it, but he pushed her away. "Take off your clothes." She quickly removed her maid uniform, then unfastened her bra as he yanked her panties down. He was excited by the sight of her large breasts (*Those gotta be D Cups)*, the nipples already hard. She dropped to her knees, taking his cock into her mouth; brushing her tongue over the head just before deep throating it. He quickly pushed her off, knowing how quickly he would cum.

Brick told her to lie on the bed. He looked her over. *Nice big thighs,* he thought. "Spread your legs apart," he ordered. She quickly complied; her thick black bush coming into view.

"Now part your pussy lips." Again, she quickly obeyed, displaying the pink interior of her now wide-open cunt. She began rubbing her swollen clit. "Quit that for now," he ordered. Then he crawled on top, thrusting his cock into her, eliciting loud moans of pleasure. He suddenly pulled out, ordering her to turn over and get on her knees. A few seconds later he was thrusting deeply, having mounted her ample backside from behind.

She continued moaning loudly; telling him to "Fuck My Pussy! Fuck My Cunt!"

He found himself frequently slipping out of her very slippery pussy when she suddenly shouted, "I want you to Fuck My Ass...FUCK MY ASS NOW!"

He withdrew from her pussy, preparing to slide his pre-lubed cock into her ass. She provided an assist; reaching behind her, she used her hands to spread it open. He was gently probing the opening with the head of his cock when she surprised him by suddenly thrusting her ass against his member, immediately engulfing the whole of it. He was amazed how easily it moved inside her ass. She made a grunting sound, then reached back, using her left hand to rub the exterior of her pussy. Her moans increased in volume - he sensed her cumming over and over. Brick, now feeling especially nasty, pulled out and went around to stand in front of her. He began ejaculating, quickly covering her entire face along with both breasts. This seemed to excite her even more as she continued masturbating furiously.

Finally satiated, she rolled onto her back as Brick headed to the bathroom to clean up.

** ** **

Kris said, "This Interview session is concluded." She turned the recorder off and closed her MacBook. The interview session included identifying data for each woman, their position in the company, what knowledge they might have about Judith's murder, and if they would like to receive any emotional or grief counseling - which they all declined.

"Okay ladies, now we're ready to have a confidential conversation about Mr. Brick Winstone."

Just then, the door opened; two women and one man - all dressed in crisp white uniforms - entered, pushing carts laden with food. Molly stood up and walked over to speak with their supervisor. After a brief discussion, she turned toward the other women and with a bright smile, announced, "Lunch! courtesy of Mr. McNeil." She returned to their table and said, "Here's our choices; roast beef, ham, cold cuts, various cheeses, Caesar salad, Italian bread, a fruit assortment, brownies, and fudge. Also Mr. McNeil has provided us with a bottle of vintage Chardonnay - *but, not really* - she said with a wink. So…let's eat!" Everybody smiled and clapped to applaud their CEO's generosity; again, proving him a very employee-oriented boss.

Everyone thoroughly enjoyed lunch; the quality and preparation excellent; so much so that Kris asked for a business card, knowing she could surely use their service in the future.

Everybody had a nice little Chardonnay buzz going on, especially Molly. The group had quickly embraced Kris as "one of their own." A high level of mutual trust had been quickly established.

Kris brought the conversation around to the main topic: Brick. "So, let's talk about this guy. *Who* he really is; *What* he's done to each of you. Who wants to start?"

Allison jumped right in. "I will. I believe I was his first *conquest.*" She went on to describe - in graphic detail - what had happened during their evening together. Further, she admitted that she had really enjoyed the sex experience, mentioning how ashamed she was for that. Kris quickly pointed out they were talking about two separate things. One, the physical enjoyment was a result of *Pandora's* effects; and two, Allison wasn't responsible for *His* deceitful behavior.

Dana spoke next, detailing her encounters with Brick, including the threesome with Sue. She quickly realized she had spoken out-of-turn about Sue, who wasn't there. Kris responded by telling them she had interviewed Sue yesterday - the reason she hadn't been included in this session. Further, Sue had said it was Okay for Dana to say whatever she wanted to about the situation. After hearing this, Dana visibly relaxed before finishing her story.

Finally, Molly pointed out that - unlike the other two- she was an honest-to-god real subject of the trial, and her involvement had gone pretty much by the book. She allowed that her anger stemmed from how Brick used his supposed best friend, Ted Dixon, to perpetrate his deceit on others. Molly apologized for being a bit more "tipsy" than everyone else, saying she believed it was a side-effect of the drug, She reminded the others that she was the only one who *Needed* the drug - what it was developed for in the first place - to cure frigidity in women. In that regard, the drug might affect her differently, especially in the long term.

This turned out to be an "ah-ha" moment for the other women. They had been so focused on his actions - the fraud and deceit - that they had lost sight of the original goal for the drug.

Next, the discussion turned to the drug itself. The effects it had on women with so-called "normal" sex drives. Allison and Dana both confirmed their earlier evaluations - that they had the absolute best physical sex of their lives, in spite of Brick's deceit. They also reluctantly conceded that he was blessed with an especially big cock and knew how to use it. Too bad it belonged to such a poor excuse of a man.

Dana related that the most intriguing aspect of *Pandora*, at least for her, was the total loss of inhibition. She felt totally comfortable talking about her sexual feelings and most intimate experiences. Seeing an attractive man, *or woman,* made her horny. Even now, days after her last dose. She said this lack of inhibition thing seemed to only concern sex. Otherwise, her moral compass was unaffected. Allison noted it was the same for her.

Molly said that she enjoyed the best sex of her life with Ted; then went on, "But what the hell do I know? I didn't have sex before Ted!" The other women burst out laughing.

"So, Kris, *What do we do* - about the sex, I mean," asked Dana. "If I'm being honest, I want to have *more* of these enhanced sex experiences. I've discovered how much I enjoy sex with a woman - not that I'm gonna give up on men anytime soon," causing another round of robust laughter. "I mean, I should feel guilty, *but I don't.* What should we do about the drug?"

"I'm a psychiatrist, Dana. From that perspective, in my opinion, I see nothing wrong. Pleasure for pleasure's sake is fine - as long as it doesn't adversely affect the other aspects of one's life. It's when it's abused, like what Brick did, using it deceitfully to obtain his own ends, then it's very wrong."

Kris continued, "You people have been honest with me, I owe the same to you. I, too, have experienced *Pandora*. My friend Robyn obtained some doses from Molly and Sue. We told our husbands about it…long story short: we spent last night having sex under the drug's influence. Including a three-way that involved myself, Robyn, and her husband, Sean. It was an extraordinarily satisfying experience for everybody."

"There's more. Yesterday, I went to Sue's house to interview her, and I acted on my bi-sexual impulse. We ended up having an intense love-making session. So, I 100% understand everything you all have revealed today. Talk about loss of inhibition. Even now - *just talking about sex* - gets me aroused." The other women nodded knowingly. "So, I believe the *inhibition* factor may be the most profound part of this whole experience. At this very moment, I would be open to having sex with any one of you (again everyone nodded). Now it becomes a *time and place* issue, which takes that prospect off the table, at least for the moment."

Molly said, "Thanks for sharing that with us Kris. As far as I'm concerned, you're now a part of this unique friendship circle." Allison and Dana nodded as they clapped their approval. "And tell Robyn the same goes for her, though I think she may already know that."

"Thank you. You've all touched my heart. What a great day this has turned out to be!" Kris said that she was very much looking forward to getting back together in the near future. "Molly, please express my gratitude to Mr. McNeil for his thoughtfulness."

. **.** **

Robyn came into the Den, sitting next to Sean. "What's up with the Open?" She asked, turning her attention to the TV.

"Just getting ready to start the second semifinal match. Who were you just talking to?"

"Oh, that was just my lover checking in," she teased. "Actually, it was LeBron. The DNA Samples Report is back from the Lab. Nothing conclusive, but apparently there was enough there to justify a search warrant for Brick's place. There's a team headed there as we speak."

"Hmmm, I wonder if he knows?"

"Probably not," opined Robyn, "he's still confined to the Mansion."

"Good, what he doesn't know won't hurt him. I'm anxious to see what they turn up."

Chapter Eighteen

Ted was sitting on the sofa, watching the Six O'clock News, "…Detective Smith said there are still no leads in the Patricia O'Brien murder investigation, again asking for the public's assistance. Anyone with information, no matter how seemingly insignificant - is asked to call the Manchester Police Department or Crime Line at 555-7171 where you will remain anonymous."

"In the Judith Winstone case, there are still no suspects, in spite of the intensive investigation. Senator Winstone, in an interview recorded earlier, expressed his frustration with the lack of progress in bringing his wife's killer to justice. For now, this is Sam McBlah reporting live from Manchester Police Headquarters." Ted heard the Kitchen door slam shut.

Getting up, he asked, "Honey, is that you?"

"Yeah, just me," confirmed Molly. "C'mon in here, I've got supper." Ted arrived just as she set the two pizza boxes on the table. "Cheese and pepperoni…oh, plus a meat-lovers."

"Smells delicious!" Ted pulled her in for a kiss.

"Wait! Let me get my coat off, you big oaf," she said, smiling.

It didn't take long before the pies vanished; both of them famished. Molly got up to put the empty boxes in the trash. "So how was *your* day, Babe?" She queried. As she set the boxes on the counter, she felt his hands sneaking around to cup her breasts, while his impressive erection pressed against her ass.

"In a minute," he muttered, caressing her tits. "First, *I want to fuck you in the ass.*"

"AGAIN?? We just did that last night. You're turning into a sex maniac; do you know that?"

**. **. **

Kris was propped up on her side of the bed, waiting for Tom to come out of the bathroom. Finally emerging, she asked him to sit in the chair for a moment.

"I've got something I need to tell you."

"And I've got something I need to tell you. I'll be a gentleman - you go first."

"Alright," said Kris, "the other night - the big *drug experiment* night - after you fell asleep, I had sex with Sean...and Robyn."

"I know," Tom said calmly, "I heard you guys."

"WHAT!!!" Exclaimed an astounded Kris. "*You Knew*? Why didn't you say something? I don't know...Hey, what are you guys doing? Or maybe, Come on and join in... *Something!*"

"You all seemed to be having such a good time, especially you. I had no idea you're bisexual. Which is perfectly Okay with me. You know I'm liberal. What the younger crowd calls, *enlightened.* Plus, you and Sean were lovers *long before* I came on the scene."

"But *Why* didn't you join in. Sean and Robyn would have loved it. *I* would have loved it."

"Because I'm not into group sex. I'm a one-at-a-time kinda guy. Just the way it is. But I have no hang-ups about it. Just was a little surprised you're bi-sexual. And I knew you'd tell me."

"*No*, I'm not bi-sexual, it was because of *Pandora.* Wait, that's not true. Yesterday when I went to interview Sue at her house, well…we had sex. And I was the initiator. She's more a lesbian. But she does like to fuck the occasional man. If I'm being honest, I do like sex with women. That desire has always lingered in the back of my mind. At the same time, I prefer a man by a huge margin - probably like 10 to 1. That said, *You're The Only Man I Prefer* - been that way since the day I met you."

"Kris, I have to ask you, *Do you love me?"*

"Yes, Tom Clipper, of course I love you. With all my heart. *You* are my man."

"Ever since your birthday, I've been thinking, *we're not getting any younger.* I don't know what the future holds, but I do know one thing. *I Love You.* Since the first time I saw you. You don't know how hard it was that first time to ask you out. Looks-wise, you're way out of my league. Anyway, ten years ago, when you said *Yes,* like the *Grinch,* my heart swelled two sizes."

Tom stood up, walked over to Kris' side of the bed, then dropped down on one knee. He looked into her eyes, and with what he hoped was his sincerest expression said: "Kris Wood, I love you so much. I want to spend the rest of my life with you. Will you marry me? Will you be my wife?"

She looked down at him, a look of pure joy spreading across her face. "Yes! Yes! I want so much to be your wife. To have you be my *Husband*!"

He reached behind, bringing a small box into view. He opened the box and Kris was dumb- founded by the size of the diamond atop the ring. "Give me your hand," Kris immediately held out her left hand. The ring easily slid onto her third finger. They both stood up and embraced, coming together for a bonding kiss. As they slowly parted, Tom gently brushed away the single tear running down her cheek. *"This is the happiest day of my life!"* She hugged Tom tightly; the two of them immersed in this moment of great joy.

****.**.****

Sean walked into their bedroom, Robyn already in her nightgown. It was an early bedtime by their standards, but they were both worn out. Tuesday didn't look like it would be much better. Robyn's phone buzzed; she glanced at the screen, then looked up at Sean silently mouthing, *It's Kris.* Then she gave Sean a jolt.

"WHAT??? SAY AGAIN!!! OH MY GOD!!!"

At this point, Sean was wildly gesturing, then pantomiming, anxious to know - *What Is It???*

"You're really getting married! I can't tell you how happy I am - how happy *we both are! Congratulations!* I'm just so excited for you both…wait…here - Sean is chomping at the bit - put Tom on!" Sean talked excitedly with his best friend for several minutes, finally handing the phone back to Robyn, who learned *they were going to be Best Man and Maid of Honor.*

**** ** ****

Sean sat at his desk, happily whistling as he scanned Tuesday's "Urgent" Emails on his office computer. Since everything that crossed his desk was marked "Urgent," the term no longer had any credible *urgency.* He chuckled aloud at the ironic pun. He looked up as the door was being awkwardly pushed open by Robyn, trying her best to balance a cardboard tray holding the two cappuccinos she had just purchased at Starbucks.

Sean got up, walking around to the front of his desk. "Here, Let me help you with that," he said, taking the tray from her.

"Damn, I almost ended up wearing those," she said as Sean set their drinks on the desk. They both laughed, in particularly good moods; a carry-over from last night's wonderful "wedding news." Before they could get settled, LeBron, not bothering to knock, came barging through the door, MacBook in hand. The look on his face proved to be an instant mood killer.

"I assume *that* is the MacBook from Brick's apartment," guessed Sean.

"No, it's mine" he said. "The Lab forwarded a copy of the video to me. And you're not going to like it. *Not One Bit.*"

Sean and Robyn exchanged ominous glances.

"They are analyzing the semen stains they found on his MacBook as we speak."

Sean set the MacBook on his desk, plugging it into power. Robyn and LeBron moved their chairs over a bit to make room for the desk chair Sean was wheeling over. As soon as they were all seated, he looked to be sure his office door was locked, then started the recording.

The opening frame showed a completely nude Judith Winstone lying on her back, legs spread wide. She could be seen talking to someone off-camera (LeBron informed them there was no audio) when suddenly Robert Landry came into view. She sat up, taking him into her mouth; after a few minutes, his head disappeared between her legs as he returned the favor.

Landry backed away slightly, the camera capturing close-up graphic images of her genitalia as her lover continued to pleasure her with his fingers. They watched as Landry climbed atop her, changing positions frequently; finally mounting her from behind, his thrusts increasing in both depth and intensity. Finally, he became still, obviously spent; shortly after, the recording ended.

The expression on the faces of both men left no doubt of their deep disgust. Robyn, on the other hand, had become highly aroused by the pornographic video unfolding before her. She had a strong urge to reach down between her legs and pleasure herself. But her shared disgust was enough to inhibit her. She made a mental note to discuss this *inhibitions* issue with Kris.

. **.** **

The three of them walked the short distance down the hall to Chief Daughtery's office. LeBron handed him the MacBook as Sean and Robyn alternately gave him a verbal preview of what he was about to see. There were no options for him. He had to view the tape before he could prepare a formal arrest warrant for Brick Winstone.

After about five minutes, he exclaimed, "That's enough! I've seen all I need to see. Turn the damn thing off!" Sean stepped over and closed the MacBook. Then Robyn, unwittingly adding fuel to the fire, told him about the semen stains now being analyzed.

Daughtery threw his hands in the air, a clear sign of his frustration and despair. "I want you three to go to the Mansion and arrest this asshole. As quietly as possible, I don't want the press involved any sooner than we have to. Me - I'm up *shit's creek*. I've gotta break this to the Senator at some point. If anybody has any ideas - any suggestions - I'm all ears." As the detectives set out on their assignment, Daughtery sank into his chair, covering his face in both hands.

** ** **

Kris sighed as she took in the panoramic view from the window of her *Manchester Medical Park* office, just across the way from her fiancée's hospital. They had parted less than an hour ago, both still basking in the glow of their impending marriage. Then Robyn called about Brick's MacBook, unintentionally bursting that particular balloon. *It is what it is,* she thought. *Have to take the bad with the good.*

Robyn had provided an in-depth description of the recording. If the DNA from the semen-stained MacBook matched the DNA they got from the sheets in Judith Winstone's bedroom, Brick is toast. But he may *never* go to trial. He's most likely insane. She thought, *Now I've got to do my best to reach a medical conclusion one way or the other. Moreover, try to pinpoint the origin of the amnesia.* Before Kris could proceed with her evaluation interviews, she had to wait for the arrest and incarceration to play out. *Bad timing. The day had started out so well…*

*** . *** . ***

The Chief sat at his desk, nervously twirling a pencil between his fingers when his intercom buzzed. It was the Desk Sergeant. "Chief, the Senator's on the way."

"Thanks, Howard." A moment later, Senator Benedict Winstone was standing in front of his open office door. Daughtery waved him in, "Come in Senator, please have a seat." As an Officer passed by in the hall, the Chief motioned for him to close the office door.

"Senator, we've known each other since we were kids…"

"Dick," interrupted Winstone, "I gotta tell you, you're scaring me."

"Sorry, Senator. There's just no easy way to say this." Without citing any evidence, like Brick's MacBook, Daughtery advised Winstone that there was enough "circumstantial" evidence to justify arresting Brick, who had moved from a "person of interest" to suspect status. The Chief, doing his best to soften the blow, lied, "I'm not convinced that he is, in fact, the perp. Unfortunately, suspect protocol for a murder suspect is very clear." Daughtery went on to explain how under the circumstances, he was required by law to arrest his son.

"I understand," said Winstone. "I only have one favor to request, Dick. I know it's a big *ask,* but could you…"

** . ** . **

Sean, Robyn, and two Manchester P.D. officers entered Brick's room. Sean walked directly up to him. "Brick Winstone, you are under arrest for illegally recording your mother's activities. Under New Hampshire law, this is a second-degree felony."

As one of the Officers searched him prior to his being handcuffed, Robyn formally read him his rights. Brick was extremely agitated and genuinely confused, but he offered no resistance. LeBron was sitting in the van parked behind the Mansion, engine running, ready for a quick exit once everybody was aboard.

Sean had decided to use the undercover Van, disguised to look like a plumbing contractor's work vehicle. Normally used for surveillance assignments, it fit the bill for this particular covert transport issue, allowing the detectives, along with two uniformed officers to arrive (and hopefully leave) without raising suspicion with the press corps.

The Officers were preparing to escort Brick to the waiting Van when Sean's cellphone buzzed. He listened intently for a moment, then exclaimed, "Stop!" Everybody stood still while he continued listening. The call ended, he looked at the Officers. "Put him in a chair for the moment and stay with him. He took Robyn aside. "Change of plans. The Chief just finished talking to the Senator. What's going to happen is…Brick will be placed on *House Arrest.*"

"…What??" Said an incredulous Robyn, not believing what she was hearing.

"Yeah, I know," responded Sean. "Apparently, Winstone convinced the Chief to confine him to the Mansion. Some modifications though. There will be two officers here to ensure he stays *inside the Mansion;* he's not allowed outside. Daughtery's going to keep it out of the news for now. So much for *equal justice for all.*"

"Yeah," cynically agreed Robyn, now resigned to the situation. "Let's not be naive, that's the way it's always been and the way it will always be."

"I'm gonna go out and give LeBron the good news. I'm sure he'll be pleased to hear," Sean said sarcastically.

**. **. **

Kris mentally reviewed what Dave Wozniak had just told her. The D.A. brought her up to date on the Brick Winstone case. *He's a sick puppy - no doubt,* passed through her mind. *But sick enough to be declared legally insane? My job is to find out if that's indeed the case. I have to call Robyn and arrange an interview with Brick. The sooner the better.* Then it occurred to her, *Damn, I forgot to tell Dave about me and Tom's engagement.*

She picked up her phone to call Robyn when it suddenly announced an incoming call. It was Robyn. "You're not gonna believe this, I was just about to call *you.*"

Kris related her just finished conversation with the D.A. before Robyn brought her up to date with the Brick arrest situation. Kris told Robyn she needed to interview him as soon as possible - Wozniak was pushing her hard since her determination regarding Brick's mental competence would play a major role in how - *even If* - they would proceed with the prosecution. Robyn asked what time Kris would like. She said 2:00 P.M. would be fine; Robyn making the official entry in Brick's Confinement Activities Log.

Chapter Nineteen

Rosita was at the kitchen table enjoying her second cup of coffee when she heard a car pull into the driveway. *Hmm, Juan is back early* (her brother, Juan; a long-haul Semi-Truck driver who wasn't due home until the end of the week). *I wonder what happened?*

The door opened. She was startled to see her sister-in-law, Maria come in.

"What are you doing here? Did you get fired?" She asked suspiciously.

"No, I didn't get fired. They sent me and Roland (the butler) home for the day. With full pay. The lady detective - the real pretty one I told you about - said that Señor Brick might be in danger and so they needed us to leave for our own safety until they figured it out."

"Maybe we can go do something," suggested Rosita.

"That's exactly what I'm thinking," said Maria. She unzipped her maid's uniform, letting it drop to the floor, leaving her standing there in a bra and panties.

"WHAT ARE YOU DOING?!" Exclaimed a startled Rosita.

"You've been after me for years to have sex with you; telling me how I needed to find out about lesbian sex - how good it is to be with another woman. *Well, here's our chance! I'm really horny.* If you won't lay with me, I'll go out and find a man that will!"

"What about Juan?"

"*What about Juan?*" She parroted. "He's, my *husband.* You're my *sister-in-law.* He's got a cock; you've got a pussy. I want to lick your pussy. I want you to lick my pussy. *Do You Want To Do This…Or Not?*"

"I don't know what's come over you Maria, but Si', Si'!" Rosita pulled off her T-shirt, then stepped out of her sweatpants. She was not wearing a bra…or panties.

The women gave each other a once-over. Maria's excitement grew as she watched Rosita's long nipples grow hard, their size in stark contrast to her small breasts. Her eyes wandered down past her flat belly to her smooth pubic mound. "I see you like to shave," observed Maria.

"And *I see* you like living in the jungle," retorted Rosita. "But what big tits you have!" She moved toward Maria, cupping her supple breasts in her hands as Maria reached down between Rosita's thighs, slipping a couple of fingers into her already wet cunt.

They kissed passionately; Maria pulling her fingers out of the damp between Rosita's slightly spread legs, tugging on her lover's arm. "Let's go," she said, urgently tugging her toward the bedroom.

**. **. **

Chief Daughtery stood gazing out his back window, lost in thought. He was feeling sad for his friend. First Ben loses his wife, then has to face the possibility (a *certainty* in his mind) his son was the cause of her death. He felt so helpless, but the facts are what the facts are. He was startled by a knock on the door. The young officer, holding a large manilla envelope, announced, "More DNA results are in, Chief."

** ** **

Kris presented her driver's license, hospital I.D. as a staff psychiatrist, and letter from the District Attorney's office documenting her appointment as a consulting physician. The Officer scrutinized her credentials, then handed them back. "Go right ahead in Doctor Wood."

Upon entering the room, she saw Brick sitting glumly in the chair across from his bed. "Good Afternoon, Brick," she said with a smile.

"Nothing fucking good about it," he replied tersely.

"I'm here to help you, Brick. Help you get your memory back. Help you learn the truth about yourself so we can figure out what happened to you and fix it. Get your life back on the rails."

Brick looked up at her, his expression slowly brightening. He believed she genuinely cared. Really wanted to help him. *Just Maybe we can find a way out.*

"The only way this is going to work is *first,* you have to trust me. *Second,* you have to be completely honest and open with me. If we can meet those requirements, I honestly believe we will have a positive outcome. Remember, I am forbidden by both medical ethics and the law from disclosing any *specific* information you provide - *unless it's directly related to a crime.* So, what do you say?"

Brick looked her directly in the eye. "I say *Yes,* I absolutely trust you and will be open and honest with you about everything, no matter how it might hurt."

"Great," acknowledged Kris, feeling relieved. "Let's get started with some basics. I believe the drug you created is a major factor involved with your amnesia. So, *Why* did you develop this particular drug in the first place?"

"*Because I could...* No wait, I'm being sarcastic. Two reasons. First, because it involves sex. Like I told you before, I'm oversexed. When I was a kid, just after puberty, I'd jerk off two or three times a day; I fucked for the first time when I was only thirteen, with a teacher at my high school who seduced me. Boy, she knew what she was doing. By the time I was fourteen, I was more sexually experienced than any other boy in the school. Like I said, *oversexed.* The second reason was more altruistic. In my senior year of college, I read a 'paper' on FSAD (Female Sexual Desire Disorder) which led me to research the subject further. I developed a strong sympathy - certainly not part of my usual character - for women with this affliction; which in turn inspired me to develop the drug I eventually called *Pandora;* which ironically turned out to be a most appropriate name."

"How so?" Asked Kris.

"Well, apparently the drug creates a healthy sex drive in frigid women, i.e. Molly Skye. In women with a normal or average sex drive, it turns them into nymphomaniacs. Hence, the analogy with the mythical *opening of Pandora's box,* both figuratively and literally. He laughed at his off-color remark. Opening Pandora's *Box - get it?"* Kris remained expressionless. "Anyway, now we are faced with the proverbial *can of worms."*

"Ah," said Kris. "And you know this *How?*"

"I drugged several women without their knowledge. Then I fucked their brains out. Correction: THEY FUCKED MY BRAINS OUT!" Brick again laughed for a moment. "Yeah, had a sore dick for days after."

There it is, thought Kris. "When did these events occur?"

"That's just it - *I can't remember WHEN.*"

Kris suddenly had an idea. *Maybe I can get to the amnesia onset point with a jolt to his psyche.* "Brick, this is going to be tough for you. I want you to watch this recording." She took out her MacBook, set it up for him to view, then started the recording (the copy Sean had forwarded to her earlier) of his mother and Bob Landry having sex.

She watched him intently. At first, he sat quietly, then began to show signs of agitation. What happened next caught her completely off guard: totally oblivious to her presence in the room, he dropped his sweatpants and underwear down to his ankles, his hard cock bobbing up and down for a couple of seconds. She was about to stop him when she thought better of it. *Let it play out, see what happens.* She was impressed by the size of his cock, but professional objectivity overcame her initial arousal. He masturbated furiously as the recording played on, ejaculating in a couple of minutes. Suddenly, he realized Kris was in the room with him and had observed the whole event. He quickly pulled up his pants, then sat back down, obviously embarrassed, a better word would be *mortified.*

"It's okay Brick, don't be embarrassed. You loved your mother in that way, didn't you. You wanted to have sex with her. You just didn't know how to ask. Is that right?"

Brick nodded to acknowledge that truth to himself for the first time. "I took the drug so I would have the courage to ask her to give herself to me."

"Wait…*what*? *YOU* took the drug - the *Pandora* drug??"

"Yes, No…not exactly. I modified the formula, trying to compensate for the male hormonal differences. I had blackouts, can't remember everything that happened after that."

"Then, the last blackout at the funeral. When I woke up, I couldn't remember anything that happened before I took the modified drug. Now I can remember everything that happened, but I still feel like something's missing."

"Brick, we have made some big-time major progress this afternoon. I think we are well on the way to getting you better. Oh, one more thing, I need to know who you drugged, then had sex with - right up to now. And it's just between you and me. That knowledge will help me piece things together."

"Sure, okay," he said agreeably. "Let's see…there was Allison - she was first - the woman knows her way around a cock; then Dana, a real wildcat if you know what I mean; we fucked twice. The second time was a threesome with Sue. That one's something else. She's got the biggest clitoris I've ever seen, really excited me - got Dana real excited, too. Maybe that's why she's a lesbian, but she sure enjoys fucking, I can tell ya that. Never fucked Molly, her being in the Study and all. Besides, she became Ted's 'girl', and he's my best friend. That's it. No…wait. The other day, I drugged our maid, Maria Sanchez. Nice body for a mature. A little Mexican spitfire - my first one - she definitely knows how to fuck, what a man likes."

"Okay, Brick. I think that's enough for one day. We've made great progress. Don't worry about your privacy, *What happens in Brick's room, stays in Brick's room!"* They laughed at her little joke. She touched him lightly on the shoulder, turned to gather her things, then left his room.

**. **. **

LeBron pulled into the police/courthouse parking garage just as all three of their cellphones notified them of incoming texts. Robyn was first to read her text. It was Chief Daughtery and read: "Come to my office immediately." Sean began to read aloud the same message on his phone when Robyn interrupted, "Same message, Sean…I'll bet LeBron's is the same too."

As soon as they parked, LeBron verified he did, indeed receive the same text. They hurried out of the garage, crossing the street to the Police Station. In a matter of minutes, they were at the Chief's door. Finishing his conversation with Dave Wozniak, he waved them in. Wozniak turned to face the recent arrivals. "Well, people, it's over. We just received the final DNA reports. The semen stains on Bricks laptop are an identical match with the DNA found on Judith Winstone's sheets and the DNA on Patricia O'Brien's body and panties. He's the killer. And raped his own mother. One sick son-of-a-bitch."

Sean said, "Sick son-of-a-bitch, no doubt, with emphasis on the *Sick* part. I have my doubts this will ever go to trial."

"Agreed," said Wozniak. "Kris Wood is interviewing him this very afternoon. Won't be long before we can make that decision. I want to thank you three for all the hard work you put in on this one. I'm proud of each and every one of you."

"I second that," said Chief Daughtery. "Now, for me, comes the toughest part of all; informing his father, the Senator."

"What about moving Brick now?" Asked LeBron.

"He's being transported here as we speak. Gonna put him in the Isolation Cell. We've been lucky with the Media so far, here's hoping that'll last just a little longer," said the Chief, fingers crossed.

**. **. **

Kris walked into her home office/computer room, setting her briefcase and MacBook on the desk before settling into the exceptionally comfortable "Captain's Chair" Tom had gifted her at Christmas. She needed to collect her thoughts - so much happening so soon; Tom's proposal (that immediately brought a smile to her face), the Judith sex recording, Brick's initial arrest for that. Now…he's charged with rape and murder, two counts of each. *Shit, I was so hopeful he hadn't done that.* Kris admitted to herself that she had surmised his guilt some time ago.

Robyn's call ten minutes prior had confirmed it. She remembered looking at a roadside billboard asking the voters to "send Senator Winstone back to Washington next November," just as she took the call. Now her strategy as a Psychiatric consultant for the D.A. suddenly has to change. No time to help him "get better." Now she had to focus on confirming his mental status. So, legally sane or insane? Unfortunately, she felt it would turn out to be the latter.

Chapter Twenty

The wine steward uncorked the very old bottle of red wine that had its origin in a vineyard somewhere in France eighty years ago. Hence, the $500.00 price tag. After Sean nodded his approval, the wine steward circled the table to pour everyone's glass.

Sean stood, raising his glass high, "To our best friends, Tom and Kris, and your coming marriage. May your love flourish, lasting a lifetime. Congratulations! We love you. Salute'."

"Thanks Sean, Thanks Robyn. I'm so happy you chose *Cassidy's Place* to celebrate our engagement. And for this exquisite wine. You know, this place is becoming a touchstone for significant moments shared by the four of us," said Tom with heartfelt appreciation.

Robyn observed, "We're just sorry for the circumstances…"

Clearly annoyed, Kris interrupted, "Not *OUR* fault. Things happen. No need to apologize, Robyn. Let's all of us just enjoy our special evening. No more *Shop* talk."

Tom raised his glass, "To our best friends; thank you for showing us what a happy marriage looks like. May we four grow old together - still best friends into our nineties…or even longer!" Smiling, the foursome clinked their glasses in toast.

Over dinner, they shared fond memories of their many experiences as best friends, basking in the warm glow of a long, enduring friendship few people have the good fortune to experience.

As they enjoyed their *chocolate mousse* dessert, Robyn said. "Please don't think of this as a *work* topic, but I'd like to know how the rest of you, especially Kris - as an experienced psychiatrist - feel about *Pandora.* Is it a good thing; like the way fine wine enhances a dinner? *Or* is using it abusive, akin to a drug addiction? The physical effect on women is just…I don't know, it's so hard to describe. When I'm under the influence of Pandora, my arousal more than doubles. I feel so *slutty*…turns me into a *whore.*"

Kris added, "I agree with Robyn 100%. The intensity of physical pleasure is just off the scale. You have to use extreme willpower to focus on anything other than sex. It's literally a nymphomaniac experience." As Kris spoke, Robyn emphatically nodded in agreement.

Sean observed, "The two of us benefit as well. Your enthusiasm is infectious. Increases my arousal substantially, always ending with a real intense orgasm." Ted quickly agreed.

"So," Ted continued, "I don't get it. Everybody involved is having a great experience. What's the harm? I mean if it's addictive like say, heroin - then we maybe have an issue. Otherwise…"

Kris cut in, "You and Sean are correct, on the surface there is no harm - especially if the substance is not addictive, which I believe to be the case. It may, however, be *psychologically* addictive. I just don't know enough yet to have an informed opinion."

"My concern, Kris," clarified Robyn, "is *The Complete Loss of Sexual Inhibition.* I mean, ANYTHING goes; you feel free to explore your deepest sexual desires. That's okay for *Normal* people like us…and Molly, Sue, Dana, and Allison. What about people like Brick? He tried to create a version for males; look how *That* turned out. He may have killed two people *because he lost ALL his inhibitions.* It went way beyond sex."

"So, you're saying we should get rid of this substance?" Posed Tom.

"No, not at all," replied Kris. "I think we have to do a thorough study; look at every effect the *Pandora* substance has, especially the inhibition - should I say, *lack of inhibition* - factor. Its intended function - reducing or curing frigidity in women shows great promise, at least in Molly's case." The foursome agreed that for them at least, *Pandora* did not present any substantial risks.

With that in mind, Robyn proposed that she and Kris might want to enhance the rest of this special evening with the aid of Pandora. She reached into her purse, retrieving two small white tablets. "You know, we've all had a pretty damn stressful day." Glancing at Kris, she continued, "I know this can be construed as rationalization, but I say why not ensure that none of today's negative events get in the way of tonight's (she added with a wink and a smile) *Whatever.*"

Kris glanced around the table, then opined, "Yeah, Robyn, *you are rationalizing;* but I, for one, Don't Give A Shit." Grinning, she stuck her hand out. "Give me one of those fucking things." Everybody laughed as Robyn, with an exaggerated flourish, presented a pill to Kris.

Both men clapped in approval as the women downed their pills with a sip of coffee. They refreshed their coffees a final time before heading out to their homes and a couple of very "happy endings" to top off this special night.

**. **. **

Sean rolled off Robyn after their third lovemaking session. "That's it, Babe," he said, "I'm done, got nothing left for ya." She leaned over and kissed him.

"You did great, Sean, I enjoyed every minute of every inch. You're an incredible lover, do you know that?"

"Thanks, Babe, look at who I'm making love to! But I gotta tell ya, I can't keep up with you *and Pandora* every night. I'm not eighteen anymore."

"No worries, Sean, I'm thinking, we're gonna invite Pandora to join us every once in a while, mostly special occasions…like this. Sound good?" She glanced over, he was sound asleep.

**. **. **

Tom looked adoringly at his fiancée. "You are something else, Kris. Brains, beauty, and a great personality. Oh, and a pretty good cook in the bargain. I feel like I'm the luckiest guy in the world!"

"You're not so bad yourself, Tom Clipper! I'm so happy I get to spend the rest of my life as Mrs. Tom Clipper." She reached over, kissing him passionately."

"Did I mention what a great lover you are?" He said, "Every time is the 'best time' with you."

"Tonight *was* special," noted Kris, "a celebration of *us*. Honestly, if it wasn't for the *Pandora* drug, I don't think it would have happened tonight. One of those rare times when I'm too focused on work. The Brick thing. So, *Pandora* definitely was our friend tonight. Anyway, I really enjoyed being with you."

"Ditto, Honey. It was great - both times. And I've got the sore cock to prove it!" They both laughed. Tom snuggled close to Kris, the pair quickly drifting off to a contented slumber.

**. **. **

The clock on the wall indicated 9:00 A.M. when Kris, Robyn, and Sean filed into Chief Daughtery's Office. D.A. Dave Wozniak, standing next to the Chief, inquired, "Where's Detective Smith?"

"He's meeting with the O'Brien family as we speak," informed Sean. "Trying to give them some closure for Patricia's murder."

"Is he telling them there is a very good chance there won't be a trial?" Queried the Chief. "That Brick is most likely looney tunes and unfit for trial?"

"I don't know Chief," answered Sean, "to be honest, I don't know if LeBron is even aware of that possibility."

"Daughtery turned to Kris. "What's your opinion Doctor Woods? You've been talking with him."

"He's definitely mentally ill. Psychotic. Most probably meets the bar for being criminally insane; effectively preventing him from being tried. I need to interview him one more time before I can reach a *legal* conclusion."

"Understood," acknowledged the Chief, "but you need to do it soon. His father, the Senator, requested a special visit with him at 11:00 A.M. Lawyers are sure to follow soon after."

"I'm ready now," indicated Kris, "if you can make the necessary arrangements."

"I'll do that right now," said Daughtery, picking up the phone.

The D.A. asked Sean and Robyn to meet with him in his Office at 10:30 to go over the case. "Oh, and Doctor Wood, please come by my Office after you finish up with Brick so we can discuss your findings."

"Of course, Mr. Wozniak, just as soon as I finish my Report."

**. **. **

Thirty minutes later, Kris was being escorted down a long hallway, at the end of which was a single cell. "Well, this cell is certainly isolated," she observed.

"Yes, it is," agreed the Officer.

When they reached the cell, he turned and left. The Officer sitting across from the cell got up. Without a word, he opened the door for her. Once inside, he closed the cell door and returned to his station across the hall. Kris determined he was far enough away so that she could confer privately with Brick if they kept their voices down.

Looks pretty disturbed, she thought. *I hope he'll talk to me.* "Hello, Brick. I won't insult you by asking how you're doing, but are you being treated well?"

"Good morning, Doctor Wood. It is good to see you. To see someone who gives a shit. So, what happens now?"

"Honestly, I'm not sure, Brick. I have to evaluate your mental health."

He answered all her questions, interspersed with nonsensical comments about women liking him only because he had a big cock when they should respect him for his big brain. He wanted to know what had happened to his mother. When Kris asked him about Patricia O'Brien, he disavowed knowing the woman. When she asked him about the *Pandora* drug, he responded, "Oh yeah, that's an idea I've had for a while now. I'm gonna get right on it. With any luck, I'll have something to work with in about a year."

She could see he was rapidly descending into a deep, dark hole of denial; one he might never climb out of. His grip on reality was literally fading away right before her eyes. *He's definitely crossed the legal threshold for insanity. He is slowly going mad,* she realized.

****.**.****

A very somber Benjamin Winstone was escorted down the same hallway Doctor Kris Wood had passed through not ninety minutes ago. The Senator knew the question he was going to ask his son. Whatever his answer, he would get him out of this mess. He was his father, after all. It was his parental responsibility. *Brick Winstone will never stand trial. I'll make sure of that.*

Upon reaching the Isolation cell, the escorting officer stood by while the suicide-watch Officer stood up, opening the cell door. Once the Senator was inside, he re-locked the door and walked down the hall with the Escort Officer. The Senator had requested complete privacy, telling Daughtery that some of the things he would be discussing would be detrimental to his reelection campaign if it got out. The Chief reluctantly agreed. He owed him that. Daughtery would not be Chief of New Hampshire's largest police department were it not for him.

Brick stood facing his father as the Officers departed. He looked at his father, not recognizing this *stranger* standing in front of him. *Who is this guy?? What does he want from me??*

The Senator looked Brick in the eye. *"DID YOU KILL YOUR MOTHER?"*

Suddenly, everything became crystal clear: *A six-year-old bouncing on his father's knee; High School graduation. "Where's Dad, Mom?"*

"He couldn't be here, had to stay in Washington; But I'm the Salutatorian of my Class, Dartmouth University for Christ's sake!"

"I know son, we're so proud of you, he just couldn't get away."

"Dad, I just developed a drug to cure frigidity in women."

"That's nice, son...got to go, someone's calling on the other line."

"YES," he confirmed. "BUT BEFORE I KILLED HER, I FUCKED HER!" He yelled, his life started passing in front of his eyes, like an old-timey silent movie, then…

His father pulled a .45 caliber Smith & Wesson revolver from his pocket, firing a single shot. The bullet struck his son in the forehead; the entire back of his skull exploded, brain matter splattering the wall behind his bunk. Brick suddenly slumped, half on the bunk, half on the floor. The Senator stared at his son's lifeless body for a few moments. He let out a sigh, then put the barrel of the gun in his mouth and pulled the trigger.

Brick Benedict Winstone   Time of Death: 11:05 A.M.

Benedict Harrison Winstone   Time of Death: 11:06 A.M.

. **.** **.** **

Six Months Later:

Matthew McNeil looked out his window at the new drug manufacturing facility now nearing completion. The CEO smiled as he reflected on Delta Pharma's recent good fortune. Completely out of debt and nearly doubling its productivity, the company was now a respected mid-size pharmaceutical business, with a growing reputation as an innovator in psychological drugs. All made possible by the generosity of one Benedict Winstone, who had died by his own hand exactly six months ago today. To honor this extraordinary man, the new facility would be named *The Winstone Memorial Building*.

He thought back to that tragic day. Benedict had murdered his son in the Hillsboro County Jail. Brick, his brilliant, but deeply disturbed son was accused of raping then killing his mother; a day later doing the same to a young women named

Patricia O'Brien. The evidence against him was overwhelming, but the likelihood of his facing trial was virtually nil; he was about to be deemed legally insane. His father, a popular New Hampshire Senator of almost eighteen years must have reached a tipping point. It was more than he could cope with given the horrible circumstances of the homicides and his now poor prospect for reelection.

The Senator must have decided on the murder/suicide two days before he followed through. That was when he changed his will dramatically. 50% of his estate was bequeathed to his wife's family; He and Brick were the last of the Winstone's. The other 50% of his considerable fortune, an amount north of 490 million dollars, he willed to Delta Pharma, Ltd. under the complete control of its CEO and primary stakeholder, Matthew McNeil.

Within the company, there was (*and still is*) much discussion about the drug Brick had developed as a treatment for sexually frigid women he had dubbed *Pandora*. There was ample evidence that Brick had ingested a variation of the drug he created for males, the intent being to increase sexual stamina. Did this drug drive him insane? Or was he *already* insane? Some female employees had been given the drug surreptitiously; none of them reported any negative affects. Molly Skye, the only trial subject, had no side effects and is still using the medication to her benefit. McNeil had otherwise suspended further testing, allowing only Molly access to *Pandora.* Or so he thought.

****.**.****

Molly Skye and Ted Dixon married on Memorial Day weekend and enjoyed a honeymoon at a beach cottage in Cocoa Beach, Florida courtesy of Dana Bryce's wealthy parents. After the honeymoon, Molly returned to college -

specifically Boston College - to get a Master's Degree in Pharmaceutical Research, fully funded by Delta Pharma. During her leave of absence, she continued to receive her full salary. Her husband also planned to resume his education and begin his first year of medical school in the fall.

**. **. **

Sean and Robyn's lives returned to the usual quiet pace they had enjoyed before the big homicide investigation. Sean kept busy with the occasional felony case; spending most of his time mentoring the new attorneys joining the D.A. Office. Robyn assumed the role of stay-at-home wife, catching up on her reading among other things. She frequently joined Molly's clique for their weekly lunches, the circle of women *still* debating the virtues and drawback of *Pandora*. None of the women had used it since the Winstone event, even though Sue had a plentiful supply of the drug. It was very likely that two or more of the women would choose to partake in the near future. The Wilders were very much looking forward to Tom and Kris' wedding in just two weeks time.

After that, Robyn was planning to write a fiction novel about the *Brick* caper. It had all the requisite elements: plenty of sex - *I should emphasize that it will be from a woman's point-of-view. Then there's some really interesting characters, not to mention a plot with a pretty twisty mystery element to it. Most of the story should be easy to write, especially the sex, since I personally experienced a lot of it. I'm definitely gonna have to change the location - maybe to Denver - and for sure all of our names - like how many Robyn Wilders live in Manchester? Plus, I'll have to come up with an Author alias. Yeah, I GOTTA WRITE THIS! It's gonna be great fun. Can't wait to tell Sean!*

**. **. **

Jean Lefleur, just coincidentally, was released from jail on the six-month anniversary of what came to be known locally as *The Winstone Murders.* After intense lobbying from Sadie Adams, Sean had convinced D.A. Wozniak to plead LeFleur's case to the Governor, who just so happened to be Wozniak's best friend. Contrary to his Council's recommendation, he granted Le Fleur a full pardon anyway. In addition, Sean secured a job for him as a master carpenter with a good friend's construction business that specialized in remodeling upper end homes. Best of all, Sadie Adams - who he owed his freedom to - and Jean LeFleur were now a couple. A "happy ending" of a different sort.

**. **. **

The *Delta Five,* the nickname Sue first suggested for their group some time ago, had stuck. Molly, Sue, Allison, Dana, and now Robyn had become thick as thieves. They met for lunch at *The Pilgrim* Restaurant most every Thursday at noon. By the end of their usual two-hour lunch, all the ladies had a pretty good buzz going, helping to juice the local *Uber* business. Lately, the main topic of conversation had turned toward *Pandora,* which had been largely absent during the subdued period following the murder/suicide.

Now they were back to the *Pandora* debate: Was it a boon…or boondoggle? Was it the catalyst behind the deaths of four people - or merely a coincidence? Had Brick unleashed something insidious upon the world? Like the legend of old, *Pandora's Box* had indeed been opened…what might happen next was anybody's guess. The group never could reach an agreement; many of the women changing their opinions over the course of a single luncheon. Sometimes twice.

There was, however, a growing consensus about one thing. Every single one of them missed the sexual highs, supplemented by the total lack of guilt conferred by Pandora. Sue had access to a large supply of *Pandora* in all its forms. And a circle of anxious, increasingly horny friends.

Be Careful What You Wish For.